# Pick Me Up

A collection of poems and short stories

Bournemouth University

Pick Me Up

A Bournemouth Writing Prize anthology

First published 2022 by Fresher Publishing

Fresher Publishing
Bournemouth University
Weymouth House
Fern Barrow
Poole
Dorset
BH12 5BB

www.fresherpublishing.co.uk

email:
bournemouthwritingprize@bournemouth.ac.uk



Cover designed by Bryony Warren

# Foreword

Thanks so much for picking me up!

This is an anthology of short stories and poems that you should come away from feeling better than you did before turning the first page. On difficult days, when the chaos and mundanity of life makes itself known, consider this book your respite; a little pick me up, if you will.

From the vast array of excellent entries to the Bournemouth Writing Prize 2022, we have chosen those that provide hope, hilarity, or simply a wholesome few minutes of reading. The world is a restless place, particularly in the previous few years, and so *Pick Me Up* was formed with the intention of gathering works that will give you a sense of catharsis.

All of the stories and poems collated in this book have been sorted into themes, allowing you to identify the kind of mood-lift you are most in need of. Each of us has their own preferred genre: while Poppy finds peace in nature, Bryony likes to lose herself in a love story, romantic or otherwise. Ailan enjoys a whimsical tale when he's feeling low, whereas Leroy lifts his spirits with humour.

That said, we've all been surprised by the uniqueness of the pieces. With these and the other genres available, we hope you will realise that pockets of joy can be found in unlikely places and that you are entertained by these wonderful words and that they

can help to turn your day around, even just a little.
Yours sincerely,

Ailan, Leroy, Poppy and Bryony
(Team biblichor)

p.s. For those who enjoy an audio accompaniment to their reading, be sure to scan the Spotify barcode on the back cover of this book to access a playlist of positive tunes compiled by the team!

# Contents

## The solace of nature



## A second of escapism

## humour as medicine

## love in all its forms

## the comfort of food



## a moment of mindfulness

# NATURE

# Lifestream

## Peter R. Storey

Ventis secundis tene cursum

She closed her eyes and swam; the water always seemed to heal. Whatever the manifold problems of the day, there was little swimming could not cure. And even on the darkest of days, when the sea wasn't quite powerful enough to restore her to perfection, she invariably felt somewhat better from having taken the time to pass, even for just a few brief moments, through its cool, though gentle, even loving, embrace.

There was something about the colours that was ever so captivating. Depending on the time of year, the time of day, the weather, and myriad other unpredictable factors, the blueish hues of the water might be cerulean, turquoise, or sapphire, anything from a sombre grey to the brightest blues and greens. Much of the enjoyment of her daily swim at Boscombe could very easily have been replicated hundreds of miles inland. The sense of playful freedom, weightlessness, and joyous fun could be found in any swimming pool. But that sublime palette of complex colours was unique to the sea.

The coolness of the water seemed to make her more reflective and thoughtful. She liked to contemplate the connectedness of the world's oceans – or should that be ocean (in the singular), for all the seas and oceans are connected. And often as she swam, on England's southern shore, her head would fill with thoughts of other swimmers who, though perhaps far away, were essentially, she always told herself: 'Swimming in the same sea as me'.

And that was it – connection. Whether to other people, to the water itself, to nature more generally, or even to her own self, the sea gave her a wonderful sense of being connected to something great. She would often remember being taught in school that life had originated in the sea. Most days there was a part of her that wondered why anyone would ever choose to leave it.

'That's enough for today; we need to be getting back!' Those words, or others to the same effect, inevitably brought a certain level of sadness or disappointment as they brought the day's swim to a close. She would never be the one to say those words herself, of course; but, sooner or later – and usually far too soon for her liking – one of the group would decide it was time to return to reality.

Reluctantly, she began her return to the sands, climbing majestically from the water as she reached the shore, looking almost like a creature of legend. She shook her head from side to side, sending a flurry of water droplets flying through the air, and began to prepare herself to face the day. Though she was always somewhat sad whenever her time in the sea had ended, she couldn't help but feel infinitely more revived and more hopeful about the day ahead than she would have been had she not been able to experience that joyful freedom and ineffable connection with the natural world.

The time between leaving the water and readjusting properly to normality was always a little strange, something of a twilight zone between the real and the ethereal, the mysterious majesty of the ocean and the banal reality of the daily landlocked routine. It was in this tranquil period that she would often experience some of her most lucid and interesting thoughts. Solutions to problems which had long beguiled her, memories from several years past, ideas of new and interesting things to do, thoughts of people, places, and emotions she thought she had long forgotten – such thoughts would surge through her brain, at an almost alarming rate, in this somewhat hazy transitionary world between land and sea. She was often very grateful for this effective buffer between her daily swim and the return to reality – a direct transition might have been just too much! Besides which, the ideas conceived in that weird in-between time were often her best.

Life outside the water always brought difficulties and complexities, annoyances and ridiculousness, sometimes to the point of making her want to dive straight back into the sea. She loved her work and her studies; but, of course, there were times when these became dull, frustrating, or tiring. She loved walking through parks, reading, and painting; but ultimately those joys paled in comparison to swimming in the sea. She loved her friends and family very much; but so often they were fraught with problems that drained her from her very core to a point which only the next morning's swim could restore. Until then, however, she had to press on through the day, sometimes good, sometimes bad, sometimes somewhat indifferent, but never anything in comparison to the exhilaration she felt when swimming amongst the waves.

On this particular morning, she had not been beset by any particular ideas of genius, as she dried herself and dressed ready for the day ahead. She had, however, been momentarily transported, in the midst of her deep contemplations, to a time and place quite removed from where she actually stood, her head filled with thoughts and feelings pertaining to people whose relevance to her life had long ceased to be of any regular or material importance. In lifelike visions far more vivid than the realest of her dreams, she laughed, talked, and cried, celebrated, and commiserated, with the figures of her past.

But it took her only minutes to get ready to face the day, and this was sometimes problematic. As soon as she had tied her shoes, the twilight zone would end. The moment those laces knotted to a bow, she would immediately and involuntarily snap out of it – back to reality. She could be mid-conversation, about to learn a crucial secret or to finally hear the punchline of a joke. She could be about to be forgiven by someone she had long thought held a grudge, or else on the verge of intimate reconnection with someone she had believed no longer cared. It didn't matter how important the contents of her mind were at that time, or how much she wished to stay in that imaginary place, the moment she was ready it was gone.

And yet she had such vivid recall of these 'sea dreams', as she would call them. Not the kind of recollection you have when you awaken from a deep night's sleep, or even a short nap, for too often those can be easily forgotten. Yes, people have dreams which make an impression, which they remember forever; but these are the exception. With her sea dreams, lasting, tangible, vivid recollection was the norm. And it was quite frequently (though notably not always) the case that their contents would influence the course of the rest of her day, for good or for ill.

The sea dreams were therefore obviously something of a double-edged sword. If pleasant visions, filled with laughter and joy, or the inspiration for a particularly good idea which would help in her work or studies, or else remedy some problem in her social life, were to be found in that day's sea dream, then clearly the day was off to an excellent start. If, however, as was sometimes the case, the dream ended on a cliff-hanger, she could spend the whole day wondering what had been about to happen. Indeed, she might have wondered about such unsolved mysteries forever, were it not for the fact that they were invariably overtaken by the considerations of the next day's sea dream, or, failing that, at the very least the pain of not knowing would be soothed away by the next morning's swim.

Even worse than the cliff-hangers were the, thankfully rare, sea dreams which she found genuinely unpleasant. Not so unpleasant that she regretted her morning swim – she would never regret that – but significant enough in negativity that they could set her whole day off on the wrong foot. Whenever these would happen, she would take the chance, if at all possible, to avail herself of a second swim in the afternoon, the thought of waiting almost twenty-four hours to resolve the matter being rather overwhelming. The embrace of the ocean was sometimes the only thing to make her feel better and, particularly as the antidote to a bad sea dream, it was always the most effective cure.

Happily, she had never in her life encountered two bad sea dreams consecutively. She was always confident, therefore, that a second swim would fix the problem. On those days when this was deemed necessary, her unrestrained joy on meeting the ocean waves was palpable. A witness to the scene would need to be heartless and devoid of emotion not to recognise the innocent ecstasy which she felt upon entering the water. The transformative, healing power was instantaneous. Not only would she feel immediately better, her smile, which was always beautiful, would be magnified to become a beaming banner of enchantment.

This intense relief – evidenced in that wonderful smile – was so powerful that sometimes the days which began with bad sea dreams would turn out to be the best days. Just so long as she could get back to the water, she would be revitalised. The second sea dream was always positive and, when set in stark contrast against the negativity of the morning, it would, more often than not, have the metamorphic potential to change the tone of the day completely. It was on those days that she needed it most – the sea. And it was a need, not merely a desire. The vast singular ocean of the Earth was to her, essentially, a comfort blanket of many millions of square miles, and she never even began to contemplate how she might fare without it.

There were only ever very occasional days when she had to make do without the nourishment of the sea. If she had to travel inland, she would endeavour to make sure this was only for a few days at a time. If ever circumstances required that she spend more than a week away from the coast, she would be practically pining for the water on her return. The gleaming smile that would radiate from her face, upon contact with the sea, after a week away, was perhaps the only time she outshone the smiles which ensued from a second swim to remedy a bad sea dream.

'It's my lifestream' – that is what she called it. And that's how she would explain it to anyone who noticed or commented, as they sometimes did, either in the positive or the negative. People would sometimes note, a few days into a sustained period without a swim, that she was lethargic, irritable, or sad – hence her firm desire to ensure such periods were kept to a minimum. Equally, anyone who met her shortly after emerging from the water – especially after a positive sea dream – couldn't fail to notice her unquenchable effervescence and joy for life. Those who knew her well enough to have encountered both versions would inevitably make the link between the two, and she was always happy to explain.

The 'lifestream' was the answer. And, for her, this was always quite intentionally written as one word. There could be no separation between the stream of water – the world's ocean – and the life which it provided. Her private journal, entitled 'Sea Dreams from the Lifestream', would make fascinating reading, if ever she shared it. But this was a deeply private volume, recounting, often in great detail, the vivid recollections of the various sea dreams her mind had cast into being. For though she always remembered the sea dreams, indeed she was positive she had never forgotten even a single one, so many of them were so profoundly important to her, that she was fearful of ever forgetting any part of them.

And this is why she had created this most private of journals. Written in her neatest handwriting – it was far too intimate and personal for typing – the leather-bound volume was a quite beautiful and inspired creation. Many of the tales were illustrated in her own hand, and often accompanied by poems inspired by the sea dreams, or even simply by the sea itself or her passion for swimming, written in elegant calligraphy with ornate historiated initials, and brought to life in vibrant colours. Quite the artist, her diary had almost the look of a twenty-first-century Book of Kells, an illuminated manuscript of the highest quality and craftsmanship. And to her, this book was almost as valuable as that elaborate collection of the gospels must have been to the monastic communities which had created it over a thousand years previously.

As a general rule, she was far more interested in the beauty of the natural world than she was in human artistic creations. And yet she was also a passionate artist, with an impressive portfolio of work. For her, art was all the more powerful when directly inspired by nature, and it was a source of immense, though intensely private, pride and pleasure to have the knowledge that the sea – her lifestream – had inspired her to create what she considered to be by far her finest collection of artworks. Had anyone been privileged to read the diary and admire its true magnificence, they would have appreciated her love of the sea and its immense importance to her in a way that even her impassioned oral rhetoric couldn't quite convey.

But as the journal was sacrosanct, always to be kept beyond the reach of anyone else, her friends and associates would only ever appreciate her affection for the ocean by the way she would talk about it. She was not shy in doing so – or at least no more shy than she was in her usual demeanour – but even the most vibrant enthusiasm she could muster could not convey the same magnitude of meaning to demonstrate her profound love of the sea as the sight of a single page of her eternally confidential diary surely would have done. Nevertheless, the fact that the sea mattered to her was common knowledge – everybody knew.

As she pulled the laces of her left shoe to a bow, she awoke – if that is indeed the correct word – instantly from the morning's sea dream and was at once fully aware of her surroundings, in a way that she simply never was on first emerging from the sea. A warm glow filled her heart as she recalled the intense yet enjoyable moments which she had shared in the dreamworld, just seconds ago, with people whom she had not really thought about in any great detail for quite some time, people who had once been so very important to her, but who had through the frenzy of life and work, laziness, or bad decisions, become unfortunately distant and remote. She resolved there and then that she would reach out and heal these divisions; this was merely one of many sea dreams which resulted in practical, beneficial actions.

As she walked along the beach, back towards reality, she considered how she might start to phrase the prose of the story she would write in her diary to document this sea dream. She began composing the first few lines of a poem to express her feelings on the subject matter and considered how she might begin to draw and paint a picture which would capture the emotions which her most recent sea dream had instilled in her. Although by no means the most profound or inspiring of sea dreams, this was nevertheless a positive one, and the sense of optimism she immediately gained by her resolution to do something positive as a result of the sea dream told her that the day would be a good one – and indeed it was. The next morning however, brought disaster.

She read the headline as if it had been designed to cause her personal offence, as though it were written for her and no one else. The simple command, 'DO NOT SWIM', was for some an inconvenience or disappointment, but to her this was everything. Or rather, it was the antithesis of everything, alienation from that which brought her connectedness to nature, to others, and to herself – her lifestream.

Most of the regular swimmers used the excuse of the putrid sewage which pervaded across the Dorset coast either to allow themselves to sleep in or else divert their energies to something entirely different. But she could not stay away whilst the lifestream ailed. Perhaps against her better judgement, she made her way as usual to the beach. She walked across the golden sands and couldn't fail to be somewhat rallied by the beauty of the sunrise. But this was not how it should be. The sea should not have been off limits to her, or indeed to anyone else.

Although certainly no expert in marine biology or environmental science, she knew, or at least she felt that she knew, that something wasn't right. The thought that people could be so careless as to think it could ever be acceptable to abuse the sea as a dustbin filled her with horror. As she reached the pier, she became completely overwhelmed with emotion. Not a selfish, insular emotion, but a compassionate, loving, caring emotion. She was aggrieved, of course, that she could not swim today. She missed that, perhaps more than she had ever missed anything. But the tears which began to flow freely down her cheeks were not tears of self- pity for the woman who could go swimming today, far from it.

These tears were a cascading waterfall of righteous anger, commanding benevolent justice. She knew that she must effect change. She didn't yet know how; but she knew she must. The sea had given her so much; but now she realised, as much as the sea can protect and nourish, it must be protected and nourished itself. She knew that she must save the lifestream. She knew that we must save the lifestream.

# On Kerrera Island

Sharon Black

This morning, I'm hiking
in the hills of Andalusia, figs dripping
from the trees,

pomegranates splitting on hot limestone rocks
amid the scrub, miles from any road.
I'm striding, dusty,

beside a Nationale
somewhere in the Midi, my hitching thumb
hooked firmly round my rucksack strap,

I've dropped behind my friends
on Rannoch Moor, damp from sweat
and midge spray, ten miles in,

another six to reach our lodge
along the Way
that keeps dipping, re-emerging.

I'm everywhere I've ever
walked alone, exhausted, aching
with some twinge or injury

and nothing but to keep on walking,
until the rawness sings
more softly, each moment passing

to the next as the spirit disengages
from its capable machine,
pulse playing out

against a drop that could be anywhere,
each step any step, no difference
between a footfall and a life.

# Silken Thread

## Molly Smith Main

Previous Life

The whiff of age and history envelopes the garment as you join
a myriad of other lives by wearing castoffs. Do they remember?
Are their minds as alive as their reminiscences? A previous lifetime
encapsulated in cloth. Love, loss, despair, elation, fear, death, truth, recreation.
Innumerable smiles, tears and breaths, bodies, warmth, DNA, spirit. Captured
souls in woven loops, recollections forgotten.

Silkworm

The delicate silkworm lives a confined life, too fragile to live in the wild.
A tiny egg emerges into larvae after ten days. After dutifully munching on
verdant mulberry leaves, the silkworm begins to slowly spin its cocoon.
Round it goes in a figure of eight, three hundred thousand times, creating a
single thread stronger than steel and over 100 metres long. Enclosing itself in its
luxurious nest, it perishes, drowning in scalding water.

## Spinning

Drowning again in bloodlike water, the silk is
transformed to a cerise pink hue.
Lustrous silken thread spun together by wizened
fingers, shrivelled worn palms
cracked by toil and time. Dry wooden wheel
relentlessly turning, pressed by
the pedal on a dusty floor. Silk spun and stored on
wooden reels, ready to be woven
in angles, warp and weft. Sold for shelter and
sustenance, sold to start again
tomorrow as bloody hands heal.

## Seamstress

The seamstress surveys the sumptuous crimson bolt,
measures her model
and cuts with a silver sharpness. Stitching again to
strop stray threads escaping, she
tucks, folds, buttons and hems. The glossy fabric
shimmers and falls,
effortlessly draping the bodily form, cloaking the torso
in raw raspberry silk.
Nipped around the corseted waist, needle-sharp and
deadly objective, stitches
uniformly, regimentally neat.

## Skirt

Worn by a youthful lady at an elegant soiree, lavish
candlelight shatters rainbow
chandeliers. Rustling opulence, dazzling bubbles,
silken cherry splendour,

lushly swishes. Music soars, and the atmosphere elevates, pinching girdle
suffocates breath, stiffly squeezing feeling of sinking. She faints into suitable
suitors embrace. On a cold and frosty nightfall, the mulberry is encircled.

Security

Pinned to the downstairs window the offcut of dark cerise silk, discarded to the
lady's maid for reuse elsewhere. Mottled and sun-bleached in abstract,
crisscrossed tape stopping shattering glass. A backdrop of theatrical fire and
searchlights sweeping the sky. No lights from within, the blackout revealed.
The shriek of the kettle and clank of the mugs, brandishing the reviving
qualities of tea. Sirens screamed, and voices raised. The razing of streets and
screech from faceless mouths.

Swished and Short

Sliced into a circular crimson skirt, swished across the floor, rocked and rolled
over a myriad of frothy lace, danced around the clock and jived until midnight.
Worn with a whorl through teenage wistfulness. Dreams of the first kiss, under
the moon, decades away. Silk transforms to stylish shortness, swinging sixties,
breaking boundaries, thighs and psychedelic swirls,

flares and platforms, disco
glitter. Silk endurance shines luxuriously as at its
dawn, longevity promising
expensive textile.

Stored

Folded away in a grubby suitcase, forgotten histories
lost in time. Materials
power from inception to inevitability, silken pink
threads fashioned for
metamorphosis. Mothball whiff, dusty darkness,
waiting for the sun, crumpled
next to handmade doilies, small, delicate, christening
robes, tablecloths of Irish
linen stained with afternoon teas from long ago.
Waiting still, silently
remembering movement, figures of eight, spinning
and weave.

Scrunchie

Passed down through generations, a treasure trove of
musty legacies. Motes
dance in sunbeams, unsealed and plundered,
rediscovering the fluidity of silk on
skin, of burnished raspberry lustre, satiny
metamorphosis into cherished
vintage. Repurposed once more into headscarves and
neckerchiefs, cocooning
elastic, and tied around hair. The silkworm's lifetime
achievement threads like
blood through the ages.

# Rural Escape Review

Laila Lock

I will take you to inland oceans
along tramways to a lone tree
holding our speech balloons
behind us like clamouring children
desperate to explore

beyond the brow
into small patchwork configurations,
passing brambled and stitched up
dramas of hope and death
where Stoat chases mouse
and the odds are thrown
to the wind
tattered nightingale singing along
humble and brown

at the cusp
where my hand a visor,
you watch me salute
the re-instated hedge guardians
in corridors of green, diffused light,
processing seasonal migrants
that vanish into repeat labyrinths

boughing propped bikes for
the rarely seen performance of
the yellow necked mouse.
Underbelly aerialist -

billed for seasonal perpetuity,
touring the rides
of shadier backdrops.
to our rave reviews.

Our day's end being bat timed,
We chase the cross-bar harnessed moons to
A back-lit station.
Counting five stars on a backdrop of English soil.

# Reunion

## Bernie McQuillan

**You should have come away with me.**

That's what his postcard said. The only one he sent her from Los Angeles and a month after they'd split. Fiona wasn't going to reply anyway but the fact that there was no return address was bloody typical of Johnny. And now he was back, dropping into their university caving club's 20th reunion as if he'd just left, his arm strung around some girl with gazelle legs that came up to Fiona's chest. What was left of it, when she took the padding away.

Aimee he'd called her, or perhaps it was just Amy, her name elongated on his Californian tongue. He talked enough for both of them which was just as well because the girl looked bored, as if a pre-dinner expedition through Fermanagh's finest cave, Pollnagollum cave, wasn't her idea of a fun night. Of course, Johnny was already tunnelling through the first passage at the front of the group, needing to show his former gang that he hadn't lost his bottle. The nurse in Fiona wouldn't just leave the abandoned girl stranded at the cave entrance so she had given her a demo, tightened her harness and watched Amy's confident abseil down to the first pitch below.

'Ok I'm down.' The rope tensed as Amy released her harness, her suddenly sassy voice rising upwards, competing with the roar of the Cladagh waterfall. It thundered past Fiona, its spray soaking her face and dripping down her back through a gap in the borrowed wetsuit. She'd lost weight in the wrong places and her scrawny neck wasn't her best look, especially next to Amy who wore her suit like a second skin. Still, Fiona thought, as she pulled the rope back up, she couldn't help but admire the girl's chutzpah. How different to the way she had been at that age.

It was only when she clipped her line onto the harness for the descent, that she discovered her hands were numbed in the chill. As she swung out into the darkness, her fingers slipped off the karabiner and she descended too fast, cursing loudly. Her feet couldn't get a grip on the slimy rocks and her nostrils flared with the pungent smell of the wild garlic in the moist cracks of the limestone. She hung there, quivering like a pendant in the Chateau Marmont.

'Are you alright?' Amy's accent was pure west coast, suggesting lazy days on Venice Beach, rollerblading to Santa Monica and drinking cocktails in the back street bars until dawn. Fiona had stayed in the Chateau once on a work trip to Los Angeles, years after she and Johnny had split. She'd had notions of casually bumping into him on the street but she discovered that no one walked anywhere in that city. Then she'd rung around as many start-ups as she could find but no one knew him. She'd given up on him then and moved to England and started again, training to be a nurse.

'I'm fine, thanks!' Fiona's voice, as firm as the former matron in her could muster. She gave Amy a thumbs-up and, ignoring her shaking hands, edged slowly down. Already the cold was sapping her strength. Her thighs squelched as she moved. How many times had she done this cave without incident but she'd failed today in front of her ex-boyfriend's girlfriend? It was hard to believe that it was only 24 hours since she'd been in her office in Saint James's Hospital, looking out over the red-bricked infirmary to the black gates and the two wheezing patients in their dressing gowns, smoking in the damp grey evening. She'd thought about going out and shooing them back onto their ward but she could understand why they preferred to be outside. Sometimes the hospital felt like a prison, she thought, glancing at the Director of Nursing sign on her open door.

It had taken ten years and long hours of training but she had finally managed to cast Johnny out of her life. Rising to the top of her profession, she'd wanted to prove to herself, or maybe to him, that she didn't need him. Bit by bit, over the second decade, the job had taken over her life. Every morning, her heels would clip past the wakening wards to the office block before anyone else was in and the only milk in the fridge was rancid. She'd pour it away, the cloud of it clinging to the base of the sink and head instead to the hospital canteen for a cappuccino. Sometimes staff would recognise her from her tours of the wards, taking royal visitors for their photos with the cutest children marred only by their nasal cannulas. The kids selected were sickly but never damaged enough to make you look away. A bit like herself. The chemotherapy had wiped her out and she knew she needed a rest. The reunion invitation had come at just the right time.

'You didn't need to wait for me,' Fiona said, her voice sounding clipped and defensive, the way she sometimes heard the nurses mocking her in the corridors. They stood together for a minute on the rocks, listening for sounds from the rest of the group, Fiona trying desperately to remember which way to go. From somewhere to the left, she caught Mike's low steady tone and Ciara's giggles and she signalled for Amy to follow her. Amy smiled at her.

'I don't think this is your thing either,' she said.

Fiona tunnelled slowly through to the next cavern, the passages tighter than she remembered, her head filled with the sound of her own laboured breathing and her helmet hitting against the roof. They finally caught up with the others in the first chamber. The pin-pricks of light from Fiona's head torch picked out the mud-spattered faces perched on the black boulders and the water dripping from the glistening stalactites. She listened to Liam telling Mike excitedly about the cavern he'd stumbled across last year, the rocks covered with flowstone, the entrance tunnel as smooth and curved as his tonsils and it was as if he'd found gold. And in that moment, in the sheer joy that Liam had experienced, Fiona felt more lonely than she ever had before.

She had flown to Belfast that morning, hired a car and driven down the almost empty motorway, calling in to see her elderly parents in the Clogher valley. She's told no one here about the cancer. At the time, work had been a distraction and she had buried herself in it after her chemotherapy sessions. No wonder her office felt more like her home than her own flat. She'd ignored the dry cough that had returned in the last month, the queasiness she put down to another damaging external investigation into maternity services. No one asked her how she was really feeling behind the lipstick and the short sleek re-growth, not even the oncologist, and so she never had to lie. After the last scan, her oncologist had been encouraging, telling her things were looking good. He couldn't say anything definite until the results were in but still.

The caving club members had gathered at lunchtime in their old haunt in Blacklion on the Irish border. Walking into Gallagher's was like being nineteen again, with the yellowed clippings of snooker finals and angling championships papering the smoky-coloured walls. Old men in cloth caps were glued to the faux leather bar stools under the green and black taps of Smithwick and Guinness kegs. There were fewer old men left now and, of course, the Guards no longer stood on the unmarked border waving you through after a night's drinking. The thin, beaky-nosed one used to lean right into Ken's car, squeaking 'you're all as full as kites, I could set fire to ye.'

Caroline was perched on a bar stool, all in black, still in thrall to the goths. Beside her, the jutting cheekbones and weathered face of Ken. Fiona had heard that he'd joined the British army, done a couple of tours in Afghanistan and had a breakdown. He had been parcelled off with a military award and a late diagnosis of post traumatic stress disorder that had left him with a facial tic and explosions of anger. Beside him, the soft Armagh tones of Liam, his violin case propped against the bar, the Guinness moistening his throat for the heavier session later. Then Mike and Ciara, the only couple from back then that had lasted. Ciara made silver jewellery now, with amethyst stones the colour of the rock pools, and Mike, who worked in the outdoor pursuits centre, a million miles away from his degree in engineering.

They'd known what they'd wanted from the start and hadn't hung about. Their kids were already at university and they were beginning their new life of semi-retirement, mountain climbing and building a cabin somewhere in France. Ciara had that sort of glow that sun beds couldn't give you, not that Fiona had been back on them since the link to cancer was established.

After a few minutes rest, Ken and Johnny led the way, climbing down steep descents and squeezing through tighter passages. Fiona limped now at the back behind Liam, having jarred her knee against an unexpected boulder. Amy powered ahead. Even the swim across the freezing lake between two chambers didn't faze her. Fiona's thoughts wandered to the hospital board meeting that she was missing, the promises her Chair would be making on her behalf that he knew she couldn't deliver. She had been the chief nurse for a decade and, in her weariness, she wasn't sure that she had anything more to give to her patients, to her team and to herself.

They descended further and Fiona crawled more slowly, like the endoscope trawling her body last Christmas, searching for the invading army of cells and finding them in her lymph nodes. The only other person around the office on New Year's Day, the day before her double mastectomy, was the dark-haired domestic, Nicole, just back from her family in Paxos. Full of excitement after her acceptance onto the nurse training programme, she had brought Fiona some Vasilopita, baked by her mother as thanks for the help she had given with Nicole's application.

'She wants you to come and stay on the island,' Nicole said, cutting a chunk of the cake and offering it to Fiona. 'I told her you never see the sun.'

Nicole shared the photos of the turquoise waters beyond her mother's kitchen where the extended family were gathered at the laden table after her grandmother's funeral. When Fiona bit into the cake, her tooth hit a small silver coin and Nicole told her that this would be her lucky year.

As they trudged on, and Fiona slipped further and further behind, she thought about those television programmes she had started watching late at night when she finally went home, where people relocated to remote smallholdings. All they did was hoe and weed and protect their chickens from intruders but the experience seemed to fulfil them in ways that Fiona had not understand initially. Their lives seemed to improve when their worlds shrunk whereas she had spent years expanding her world, seeking happiness by reaching out to more and more people. She had hundreds of followers on her social media accounts and had to keep feeding the beasts, thinking up different ways of saying the same thing. It had become work, this twenty four hour media presence, alongside the great burden of responsibility for the patients and the staff. These people on television were full of joy in their new simpler surroundings. Recently, she found herself wanting to emulate them.

It was the sort of fulfilment she had imagined came from having children. At one point, she had anticipated that life with Johnny, her calm steadiness mixed with his charm. But she no longer had the energy for that. Instead, she imagined an alternative life, maybe living on the Greek islands, drinking frappé at a beach tavern and watching the sun set over the bright blue fishing boats nestling in the harbour.

Not looking behind, nor ahead. Just being. Enjoying life.

Finally, she emerged, exhausted, into the deepest chamber with its creamy calcite curtains and the jagged teeth of the stalagmites like a giant's smile. No one had noticed her absence. A line from Yeats' poem came to mind as she leaned heavily against a rock, one that Fiona hadn't thought about in years: 'I hear it in the deep heart's core.' She thought about Yeats' grave at Drumcliffe, not forty miles from where they stood. His remains might even have leaked into the mountain water that flowed down into Glencar Lough and through the cave system into this passage, just like the soul of Nicole's grandmother on her journey to paradise.

Caroline produced bars of chocolate from the emergency box and passed around cartons of juice. Fiona's feet squelched in her ruined trainers. There was a steady hammering in her head. Her arms were so cold and weak, she could barely lift the drink to her mouth. She watched Amy move away from Johnny to examine the rock pearls shimmering in the far corner.

'Did you ever think you should have come away with me?' Johnny was beside her, his thighs not quite touching on the rock, his breath filling the space between them. In the light from her head torch, she saw how straight and white his teeth now were, so different to the crooked smile he'd had before that had caught her attention that very first day at university.

She wanted to say something witty, maybe even something honest, but when she searched her mind, nothing was there, only utter weariness. She had thought about him for years after he'd taken off, wondering if it could all have been so different. And what had they fallen out about anyway? Whose career was more important, something like that. She wanted to say it was irrelevant now. Too much water under the bridge. She began to feel even colder and she started to shake, unable to get a word out. Her throat ached and the dry hacking cough returned, echoing around the chamber.

'Dad, come and see this!'

Johnny's hand brushed against Fiona's arm as he moved away. Across from her, Fiona saw Caroline and Ken exchange glances and she knew they were thinking the same thing as herself - Johnny hadn't waited about, then, if this girl was his daughter. Ken passed her his hip flask and she lifted it to her lips and drank something like brandy that shocked her cough into submission and made her throat sting. She felt the searing heat hit her belly and pain radiating throughout her body.

It was a few moments before she realised that Caroline was asking her if she was all right. She couldn't speak, only shake her head. She watched Caroline signal to Ken that it was time to go. They were, Ken said, suddenly purposeful, exiting by a different route. She could hear it in his voice, some reminder of life on the edge, ricocheting between survival and disaster. She followed him, listening to Caroline's soft words of encouragement behind her and silently weeping when, after climbing upwards for half an hour, a shaft of light shone obliquely into the cave. They came out into the fading summer night and the loud chirping of the crickets. Fiona collapsed onto the grass, gasping in the air.

'You were fantastic,' Ken was saying to Amy, 'for a first timer. You put us all to shame.'

When they were changed and back on the bus, Fiona checked her mobile. There was a message from her oncologist telling her to ring the hospital urgently. Any time, day or night. She looked up and saw Johnny watching her, a smile playing on those perfect lips. Later in Gallagher's, he said she was the first to know, that he was leaving California. Amy was going to university in London in September. He was selling up, finalising his divorce, getting ready to live again.

'It's time for a change,' he said, his eyes on her face. 'I'm coming home.'

Fiona nodded absently, warming her hands on the hot whiskey, her mind full of Nicole's photographs and her mother's offer of a bed on Paxos. She knew that, up close, the Aegean was the deepest hue of aquamarine. She would explore the caves at Amphitrite, diving through the sea's emerald green, cobalt and navy blue depths.

Not for her the stark grey rock of Yeats' grave and the sodden Fermanagh hills but the gypsum-covered underworld of the sea goddess. Her reddened fingers tightened around the glass and she knew that, from now on, she would only live in colour.

'I'm coming home, too,' Fiona said and tipped her whiskey glass to his.

# ESCAPISM

# Autumn Skies

## Michael Gaines

The funeral pyre burned hot. Its flames seemed to reach the heavens. None could see the twinkling stars above them, nor the full, pale moon. All that mattered was the pyre. The light shimmered from the armour of those around Gawain. He watched in the reflection of breastplates and helmets as his father's body burned.

When it was over, many lingered for quite some time, whispering quiet prayers. They stood in silence as the night sky melted into the dawn. Despite the chill, Gawain stayed even longer. He was the last to leave. When he turned his back on the smoking coals, he knew he was not ready to return to the castle. He needed to sit down. Somewhere he could think. So, he made his way east, up the tall hill, where he knew he could rest by the old oak.

When he got there, he saw that he was not the only one reluctant to return to the safety of the city walls. An old man sat by the tree, looking out across the valley below as the sun rose before him. Gawain knew the old man well. They all knew him. He had been old even in the time of his grandfather, and never seemed to age a day.

Gawain said nothing, sitting beside the old man, joining him in silent reverence of the breathtaking view. The edges of clouds began to light up with an array of pinks and yellows, and the inky blue of the predawn sky grew paler with each passing moment.

Eventually, the old man said, 'Autumn skies.'

'What?' Gawain asked, when the old man deigned not to elaborate.

'Autumn skies,' the old man repeated. 'I find them the most beautiful of all. There is something about them. I can't quite put my finger on it. The sun hangs low all day, hardly higher than two hands from the horizon. It makes everything seem stretched. Drawn out. Prolonged.'

'Prolonged,' Gawain said back to him, 'but not stopped. It will still set.'

The old man nodded. 'And it will rise again on the morrow. Nothing ever ends, Gawain, Son of Galahad. It only rests. Like the tide, the world breathes in a constant rhythm. The cycle resets. Nothing stops. Winter will arrive by week's end, but spring is just around the corner.'

'And what of the Round Table?' Gawain asked. 'My father was the last. Summer is over for Camelot.'

The old man took a deep breath. Merely being in his presence made Gawain feel a strange sense of peace.

'Legends die every day,' the old man said. 'But, for every legend that passes into the next life, another is born. It is the cycle beginning anew. Their memory will last for all time, and we will forever honour the sacrifices that they made, and the great feats which they achieved. Still, it remains the duty of the younger generations to do better than those that came before them. Do you think that Arthur and your grandfather were the first legends to walk these shores? Do you think they will be the last? Do you think they set out to become heroes? No, Gawain. They saw the problems in their world, and they dedicated their lives to finding solutions. In many ways, they succeeded. But, in others, they failed - as we all inevitably do.

Not all battles can be won, and this world will forever have need of heroes. They are our guide. Examples to follow.'

Gawain dropped his head to his chest. 'I will never be like them. I know people expect me to be. My father was the greatest of us all. The things he achieved... it is impossible for me to be greater.'

The old man shook his head. 'True heroism is not achieved by those that seek it out. It is achieved by those who intend only to do good in the world, for the sake of goodness itself. To leave things better than they found them. It is the choices we make that determine who we are.'

The old man turned to face Gawain, his long beard scraping the collar of his robe. 'A man that sets out to fight a dragon is not a hero, Gawain,' he continued. 'That man wishes nothing but glory for himself. But the man that hears a child's screams from a burning building and charges into the flames, despite the risk to himself ... now that is a true hero. I see such heroics every day, and they have nothing to do with grails and magical swords. I see women go through excruciating pain to bring children into this world. I see old men offer their cloaks to children when it is cold. It is the small things that make you who you are. The small things are what make you capable of the grander ones.'

Gawain sighed. 'But how will I know if I'm doing it right? How will I ever achieve the dreams my father and grandfather reached for? They fought so hard to make those dreams possible for us. I don't think I'm strong enough to achieve them.'

The old man smiled. 'Oh, Gawain. You will never achieve them. The sooner you accept that, the better.

Dreams are dreams. They are immaterial. They are impossible. But, does that mean you should never try? No. Aim for the stars, and you may only reach the moon. But, aim for the moon, and you may not reach it all. Do you understand?'

Gawain nodded. 'I... I think so.'

'Good. Perfection and ideals will forever be out of reach, but you can get close. That will be good enough. All that matters is that you try. I have always felt that intentions mean far more than results. Be kind to those around you, Gawain. Listen to them. Help them where you can, but remember to also help yourself, too. A man at peace can do far more for others than a man at war with himself. I will leave you to ponder that.'

'Leave me? You mean, you're going back to the castle?'

The old man shook his head. 'No, I think not. I think it is finally time that I joined my friends.'

Gawain felt a tear suddenly roll down his cheek. 'You cannot go. Not now. People need you. *I* need you.'

'No one has ever needed me, Gawain. All I have ever done is given them a little push in the right direction. They would have gotten there on their own, eventually.'

Gawain did not think his heart could handle another loss, but he knew nothing he could say would change the old man's mind. 'Aren't you scared?' he asked him.

'Of death? No, my boy. I have had many adventures in this life. I am nothing but excited to see what the next one offers. Perhaps I'll even be a bird. Wouldn't that be something? I've always wanted to be able to fly.'

Gawain tasted the salt of yet more tears, wiping them away with the sleeve of his shirt. 'What will we do without them? What will we do without *you*?'

The old man shrugged. 'The same thing you've always done. Live. And that's what you must do, Gawain. Live. And live well. Know that, though there is great evil and suffering in this world, it is made less each day by those that choose to be kind. The wealth of unity has forever been the message I have tried to teach. But, remember ... you will never fully banish evil, Gawain, and you would not ever wish to. Without darkness, light has no meaning.'

The old man turned to leave, and Gawain leapt to his feet.

'Merlin?'

'Yes?' the old man said, looking over his shoulder.

'Thank you. For everything.'

The old man smiled. 'You are most welcome.'

With that, the old man vanished, strolling down the western side of the hill. Gawain looked back to the rising sun, and moved to stand beside the ancient oak. The old man was right.

Autumn skies were the most beautiful.

# Night and Day

Brad Petrie

I will never forget the night I first heard it. A delicate harmony whispered through the air from afar. It was like nothing I'd ever heard before. The sound kissed the breeze and brought a warmth that alleviated the bitterness of the night. A song sweeter than the birds. Clearer than a waterfall.

When I was young my parents and I were travellers. We lived in a small carriage which we'd move from town to town, only travelling at night. We never stayed anywhere too long before we had to pack what we had and be back on the road. I was never schooled but they made sure I could read and write. They taught me to never go out during the day. Daylight is poisonous, strictly move in the dark. So that's what we did. I can't recall many memories from my childhood, it feels like an eternity ago. A distant memory that fades ever more each day. I was 18 when I last saw them both. We were staying in a cave in a remote hillside surrounded by enormous ancient trees and crashing waterfalls. We'd never stayed this far out before. I rose in our cave in time with the moon like we always did but my parents were nowhere to be seen. The carriage was gone too with no explanation. I haven't seen them since. Why would they leave me here? Time moves fast when you live alone in the wild, I'm not sure how long it's been since the day they left; so long I lost count of my age too. It can be lonely at times, even the animals run from me. When the moon comes out and I awake, they hide underground or in the trees out of sight. Sometimes I worry my parents felt the same as the animals and I scared them away.

There was nothing unusual about the night I heard it. I awoke from the same cave in the hillside as the poisonous sun went down and the moon was high in the sky. The cold thin air seeped through my skin and rattled my bones. The small scurry of mice or flapping of wings in the trees above was heightened tonight. After sleeping for what felt like a few moons, a supernatural urge takes over your body, pushing you in the direction of food. My throat was gasping for any drop of blood I could get my hands on. Now I understand the poor animals' fear. My parents would always catch their food and leave me the blood because they knew it was my favourite. That night an unsuspecting deer was drinking from the river at the nearest waterfall. They didn't finish a sip before I sunk my teeth into its warm neck. It squealed and jittered in the running water before giving in to its inevitable end. The remains were dragged back to my cave where it would lay on the cold wet floor before my next feed. An overwhelming sense of guilt overcame me after every feed; with the little memory I had, I could never recall my parents letting me feed this much. As I've gotten older, I crave animals' blood more and more. The guilt of them seeing me now always brings me to the one spot I feel comfortable.

Beyond the waterfalls and away from my cave, there was a hill. This hill was the highest point for as far as the eye could see. The view from here was remarkable, you could see the icy wind flowing through the dips in the land, rustling even the highest leaves in the tallest trees. Beautiful deep-yellow flowers were scattered across the grass all the way up the hill and at the very peak lived a single apple tree. Its blood-red fruit lay around its base and across the grass which mingled with the flowers to create a collage of colour. I found comfort in this tree; we have a lot in common. All alone in a land we didn't choose to live.

Then I heard it.

It broke the deafening silence and rolled gently up the hill to where I lay. For a second, I felt hypnotised, the cold left my body like I'd been gifted a hug from an angel. As an apple fell from the tree I jumped to my feet and scanned the land beneath me. A beaming light came from a small shack amongst the forest on the opposite side of the hill. This wasn't here before. How long did I sleep this time? Recently the concept of time has been fading quickly, I couldn't keep track of how many moons had passed since I last left my cave but other than my parents, I had never seen another person here before. Could it be them? Then I saw long blonde hair belonging to the angel draped out of the window and blowing softly in the wind. We seemed to be of a similar age. Her skin was as golden as her hair, it reminded me of my mother's. My pale veiny skin was always different but it never seemed this cold and empty. She sat dreamily on the window ledge and hummed mystical spells into what looked like a violin. I'd read about them but never seen or heard one before. I sat and watched until the night began to retire; a slither of sunlight peeked over the horizon and singed my skin back to reality. Who was this girl?

I came back for the next three moons in awe of this girl trying to work out who she was and how she made such mesmerising songs. That was until one night just before the sun rose, the girl looked up at the single tree on the tallest hill and caught me gazing. We stared at each other for a moment, her river-water-blue eyes fixated on mine. For the first time in forever I felt like the thing looking back wasn't scared of me. She darted from the window and I scurried like a mouse behind the apple tree. Peering between the branches at the shack I saw the girl stood between two men, much bigger than her. The men came out wielding arrows and spears.

'Are you sure you saw it?' the burly men asked hurryingly. The girl paused for a second, looked back up at the tree, fixated again.

'No,' she lied without taking her eyes from the hill.

'What have we told you about going outside at night? It's dangerous. Now, come inside,' the tallest of the two demanded.

'The night? Dangerous?' I murmured to myself puzzlingly. The light where the girl sat went out and I retreated back to my cave.

***

It must have been many moons before I went back to the hill. I was still shaken by the men who protected the girl. As I climbed up the great hill, I noticed some of the apples that had fallen from the tree had been eaten. I looked around for more clues until I came across something lodged in the roots of the trees. It was a violin, the same violin the girl had been playing. I picked it up and began to play. A harsh screech echoed through the valley. With that, the girl's light flickered and there she was, holding a violin of her own. She looked up at me with a smile and began playing. This girl was truly an angel. I came back to the hill every night to watch the girl play. The more I watched, the more I fell for her. We lived such different lives, but we had made a connection through music. I practised and practised in hopes that one day we could play together. The girl could only go out during the day when the blistering sun was high in the sky. She was otherworldly but to me she was perfect.

Every so often the girl would leave me letters to read when I got to the hill. Her name was Rose. She told me all about her days when I wasn't around and left drawings of the two of us playing our violins together. She explained how her brothers would not let her out at night as there were deadly creatures that lurked in the forest. I wrote back to tell her I'd never seen these deadly creatures and that her brothers were wrong. We wrote letters and played our violins from afar every night. As the moons went by, I got better and better at the violin but never as good as Rose. I could never get bored of watching her play, each night was as beautiful as the first. I never wanted it to end. The cursing crack of sunlight in the horizon forced me to leave the hill away from Rose. If only she would see there were no creatures out here. I have never hated the sun more than now; it was the only thing stopping us from being together. While I hid from its rays back in my cave, Rose clouded my mind. The sweet sound of her music played on repeat in my head. I imagined how her golden hair would feel between my fingers, seeing her baby blue eyes flickering in the light instead of the pitch black. That was until one night, she left another note. 'In three nights' time, meet here, love Rose x'. Could this be a trick I wondered? Could her brothers be trying to lure me into a trap? I waited for her to appear, but for the first time she never came. The light in her shack never flickered and her music never played.

'Three nights time,' I muttered. 'three nights time'

On the third moon I decided to make my way to the hill. I had to be cautious this time, it could be a trap after all. As I slowly climbed, I could hear that unmistakable sound coming from the top of the hill. Then I saw her. Elegantly sat at the base of the tree, her pearl white dress and wavy hair blowing in the wind. I moved closer until we sat side by side.

'You're not that scary for a vampire,' she said.

# Calico

## Everett Jay Buchanan

I met a woman from an ancient land;
Hair dishevelled and covered in beige powder.
Skin as black as the winter sky,
eyes narrowed and full of armed tragedy.
A skull under her hand;,
she runs through the desert.

Half- covered visage laid bare to be covered;
pretty flowers, but not for her.
Wrinkled lips from singing at the sky, a passion read in her posture.
There she stood, a queen amongst eagles.
Cacti raising, a sole pole stretched and eroded from the ground.
A boundless sky above;
the finite horizon stretches.

The pole pierces the head,
a white creature with antennae,
like an alien stretching out.
A hollow mind,
empty to rot and judgemental destitute eyes.
Lips bound by a calico;
a rose with a bow, flying like a kiss into the lonely summer air.

We stand alone.
Me and her.

Her and the head.
Adorning the grave with the flowers she wishes to have
I stand there too,
wishing for a kiss by the same calico.
The queen of knights and her desolate kingdom,
An idol amongst tangerine skies and nights marked with a hundred stars.
An idol amongst the vast cape of red dust that will soon bleed through the ossein.

# One who Flies

## Felix Fennell

They have grown older again, Feiyu thinks, peering over the rim of his cup to study the faces of the only two people he has ever called 'friend'. There are new imprints in Song's face this time, fresh little creases of crow's feet in the corners of his eyes and a furrow to his brow that sits heavier than it used to. He frowns deeper now, his face set into an expression of displeasure that Feiyu knows is not reflective of his feelings. In their youth, lifetimes away from where they are now, his face hadn't seemed quite so severe, though his looks have only aged well in the meantime. Smiles have always suited him better than the grimace he puts on these days, but Feiyu knows better than to wish for things of the past.

The rice wine in his cup still tastes the same; a familiar burn warming the tips of his fingers and the hollow of his ribcage. Once, he would have filled the silence with chatter and gossip, his voice bubbling over the table between them and reaching Song and Huan over top of what would have almost always been a playful dispute. He had never stopped them in their bickering, and found amusement curled his lips at the way they, insulting one another, still transparently treasured the company.

Now there is only the silence and the quiet noise of cups clacking gently against the table when lowered after a sip of tea. It should unnerve him more than it does, but he more than anyone can appreciate the ways in which they've changed these past fifteen years. It no longer surprises him to see the ways in which the three of them have failed to remain impervious to time, and, in a way, he's come to appreciate the evidence that he has known these two almost as long as he's known himself. Just as he has witnessed them go from boys to men, they have seen the same of him. The thought brings him both comfort and an unfamiliar nervousness, the kind of which he hasn't felt in years.

The sun above them is hot, and though they have come to the city for the spring with the express purpose of seeking this warmth, Feiyu remains grateful that his own hometown is much cooler. Across from him, Huan is tentatively pouring a cup for Song, trying very hard to ignore the way Song looks at him. There's years worth of hatred and insecurity behind his eyes, and Feiyu swallows back a sigh at the sight of it. If only they were the type to sit and talk about their history, he wouldn't feel the need to interfere like this, calling them all to such a meeting. Still, he knows they're older and wiser than they used to be, and had he attempted such a reunion even a year before it was time, Song would already have thrown himself bodily across the table and fixed his hands around Huan's neck.

He doesn't quite know how to talk to them, either. Not really, not anymore, and the horror of that is something fierce. It settles into his bones with a quiet agony, and were he any other man he might mourn something like that loss of understanding. He studies his reflection in the cup, in the little puddle of liquid still inside, and finds a tiredness hanging beneath his eyes that surprises him. This meeting was a leap of faith, more than anything, an attempt to rebuild the bridges they had all burned with one another over a decade ago when they were young and angry and not yet cognizant of the world around them.

'Come on, you can't be angry with me forever. Aren't I graciously pouring your drink for you now? Surely you wouldn't begrudge me this.' The floating, light tones of Huan's teasing filled the space between them, and Feiyu allows himself to huff out a laugh at the familiarity of it; even as Song turns that fierce glare on him. In return he offers a smile, unaffected. Song's bark was always worse than his bite.

He scoffs, turning his face pointedly away from his brother and turning his nose upwards. 'Do whatever you want.' Is what he spits out, and Feiyu can do little more than bite back the laughter he feels tempted towards.

'So stubborn, still.' He chides, voice gentle even in its amusement, and Song fixes him with a look halfway between affronted and embarrassed. His cheeks are flushed, and Feiyu remembers that *Ah, this is a man who has always blushed easily.* It's just as unexpectedly endearing on this man in his forties as it was on the boy of seventeen, when they had met, and no less fun to observe. There's a prolonged pause between them, during which even Huan's hand stills after pouring Song's drink for him. He lowers his eyes to the table under the weight of their stares, suddenly self-conscious, and takes a small sip of his wine. Mentioning the past was not taboo, exactly, but it must have been an uncomfortable reminder that he, himself, had known them.

Their hands have all been stained red by now, with all the years of fighting and scheming they have endured, but Feiyu knows that of the three of them, he is an outlier. He is someone the common people tout as untrustworthy - flighty as the birds he keeps and no less vicious when the mood strikes him. A snake in the form of a man, some say, and he has heard their whispers as loudly as he has heard their shouts. It remains water over his back, more or less, but he knows the distrust of their people filters upwards, and there are traces of it in the eyes of his once-friends. It stings just a little more than he had thought it would, prepared as he had been to see it. But he has changed, as have they, and he has known for many years that this mistrust is something of his own design, and he cannot begrudge people for falling into the traps he himself had set for them.

The stars are as far away as they have always been, but as he takes another sip of his wine, Huan places his palm flat on the table and leans his weight across it, towards Feiyu. 'What hasn't changed about us, I wonder.' He murmurs, and Feiyu takes it for the insult it must be, meeting Huan's sharp eyes with a pleasant curve of his lips. He can feel Song watching them - watching him - closely, and the thought of these two estranged brothers coming together to display so shamelessly their wariness towards him almost makes him laugh.

He knows when his smile takes on a sad quality, because the lines of Huan's face relax a little, softening around the edges. His friend sighs, and withdraws to his own seat beside Song, and Feiyu watches the silent conversation pass between them. They're deciding among themselves how to treat him - as the friend he used to be or as the stranger he has become. He knows he won't push them one way or the other, content to watch them come to their own conclusions.

'Feiyu,' comes Song's voice, deep and smooth and reverberating across the distance between them. Feiyu allows his eyes to slide shut, against himself finding comfort in it, 'You look well.'

'Thank you,' he smiles, 'the sun is warm, and this town holds enough joy from my memories to set me at ease.'

'Your tone is as light as ever, Feiyu.' Huan interrupts them with a grin, though its corners belay his lingering bitterness, 'Had this place lost its shine, surely it would have been your jaws closing around it?'

The chuckle that escapes him is unrestrained, 'And you are as amusing. I have never taken that which I was not owed.' Huan's grin widens, but the bite of it has shifted, and Feiyu feels vaguely as though he has passed a test.

'Not even life?'

'Not even that.'

Across from him, Song scoffs, but does not protest. They dare not begrudge him his personal vendetta, and he silently feels grateful to them both for that. It's still something he feels deeply about, and though there is a lack of trust between them, it seems he is not the only person trying their best here. Huan's palm retreats from the surface of the table, and he leans back to recline in his seat.

'What do you plan to do now?' Song asks him, his fingers twitching slightly around his cup, and Feiyu sighs. The weight of his actions is heavy, but he has walked with his back bowed for too long, and he knows this friendship is too old and too new at the same time for lies.

He sets his cup down on the table, and turns his face towards the sun.

It warms his cheeks, and he feels the tension seep out of his shoulders the longer he basks in it. His friends are quiet, perhaps watching him, and perhaps watching each other.

As a boy, he had raised birds free from pretty cages, and they sang for him when he was lonely. Before anything, he had befriended his birds in the trees and the rabbits on the forest floor. Wild things, unkept and unrestrained, free to fly on the winds that ruffled his hair and his shirts. He had scraped his knees climbing the trees after them, and his hands still bore the scars from too-sharp bark beneath his palms as he climbed until the branches could not bear his weight, and broke beneath his hands.

A paintbrush and canvas were the friends he had made in those days, other than the wildlife, and for all that his childhood had been an unrestrained whirlwind, the unchanging face of the wild and its creatures had brought him comfort. The sky remained the same wherever he was, though the shape of its clouds was changeable, he had found freedom underneath those streaks of white and blue. The trees did not know his name, and he knew nothing of them, but they had housed him when the sky cried, and they had cradled him in their branches when he had done the same.

He faced the sun in those days, unflinching, and he had always smiled to see it. It brings him the same comfort it did then, though his company consists of men and not birds.

Huan and Song have been irreplaceable to him.

They are both older by little more than a year, and for a long time they had babied him. Not to the point of belittling him, but he had felt acutely the way his birds must have as he himself fussed over them and made sure they were well-fed and safe. They had been the first to treat him with care, and as a boy he had believed it would last.

Much later, when his efforts had been acknowledged, and the body of his once-friend lay at his feet, the tiredness that washed over him had left him drained. His friends had stared at him, with his red hands and his red face, and they'd turned away. He had never held it against them, and he knew he never would.

He smiles, and for once it is not fake or heavy with regret. Today is warm indeed, he thinks, and turns back to his friends. What will he do? He has no home to return to anymore, and no one to welcome him back. This tentative truce between them is too fragile for him to ask for help, and it is not in his character to lean on others even if he knows very well it would be better if he did. His friends are waiting for him to answer, and Huan smiles back at him when he faces them again.

'I think I'll travel.' The answer he gives is tentative, and he knows he must sound more fragile than he means to, because Huan's smile turns sympathetic. He reaches across the distance between them to take Feiyu's hand gently in his own, and the harsh lines of Song's face soften.

'When you return, come visit. It will be lonely with one less person to tease.' Is Huan's immediate response, and it prompts a laugh from all three of the men around the table. His hair is greying at his temples, Feiyu notices, and he chokes on a sob with the next breath he takes. The road behind him has been long, but even as the evidence of their ageing begins to show on their refaces and in their hair, Feiyu thinks this little trio of his is something he will not neglect to treasure twice. They aren't getting any younger, after all.

Overhead, a sparrow flies towards the sun.

# HUMOUR

# Consequences

## Sharon Savvas

By late summer, the days slow and the nights swelter. The air, thick with pine-scented resin, myrtle and thyme, induces languor in both mortals and immortals. It drives Hermes mad, because for him it is not business as usual. It is not business at all.

In the busy seasons, guiding dead souls and delivering the Gods' missives is 24/7 and Hermes has been known to mix the two up. Like the time he confused the golden bow and arrows wrapped in pale silks from Lord Ares to Lady Artemis with the dead senator wrapped in pale linens for dispatch to the Underworld. Uncle Hades was delighted with his new toys, but the tantrum Lady Artemis threw after she unwrapped a corpse instead of the weaponry she'd ordered, meant Hermes had to wear his helmet of invisibility for a month.

But this time of the year, messenger business is slow and fewer souls need a guide to the Underworld.

On the golden plains, mortals cling to life, loathe to risk life or limb or to expend energy beyond the necessary; to eat, to fuck, to bathe, to...to..., well there isn't much else.

Preferring the shade of their villas to the shadows of Erebus, the aristocracy hide from the onslaught of sun. They sleep late in their privilege, idling away the days protected by cool stone and deep inner pools, waited on by houseboys and slaves. By night, serviced by concubines, of all persuasions, the elite drink the last of the year's wines and gorge on the benevolence of the season's abundance.

But in these burning, brutal months, nobody, not even the hoi polloi, worked hard. The prevailing exhaustion was not the malignant sort, but the kind that came from nights rousing in inns or rutting in brothels tended and pimped by porn-shepherds, who sold their *obols* of flesh and who never, ever went out into the light of day. It was the exhaustion of indolence. Some called it a little gift of the gods, this time when nobody divine or mortal could be arsed.

The Gods don't meddle during summer, preferring a bit of R&R in their cool mountains and leafy woodland retreats. Hermes, a child at heart who needs constant distraction and is restless in his boredom, jumps when Dad sends a white raven to summon him. He slaps on his wingèd sandals and helmet, grabs his satchel and caduceus, leaving his tortoise and rooster to their stir-crazy madness, to fly to Zeus's latest super-deluxe, razzamatazz sanctuary on Mount Olympus. Mount Olympus where Hephaestus has built the Gods their Very Serious Convening Palace. Because of his inferiority complex and doomed to ungodly imperfection by a very gammy leg, Hephaestus had gone way OTT and out the other side to curry favour and avoid offence. Piling on the sycophancy, he plastered the palace with gilded depictions of their attributes, feats, and frankly bullshit beauty.

Following the raven's slipstream between the colonnades, Hermes baulks his first landing at the sight of all twelve flashing, dashing, cue inverted commas, GODS. Elevated by three flights of white granite steps, surrounded by pink and black-veined marble columns, they loom, swollen with self-importance on their thrones. He circles around for a second approach but as he comes in to land, perspiration, brought on by the speed of the flight and trepidation at the sight of the assembly, stings his eyes. He fluffs touchdown completely, stumbles, stubs his toe, tumbles forward and pulls up just short of smashing into the lower step of the sacred Stairway to the Heavens.

Twelve pairs of delusional eyes watch Hermes right himself. He straightens his helmet. The wing on his left sandal flaps like a broken shutter.

*Bugger, that'll cause problems.*

Shamed by the tittering and sniggering, he fumbles with it.

'Such a smooth operator.'

*Hera!*

Like all of Zeus's offspring not born of her self-appointed golden loins, Hermes suffers from his stepmother's spite. He is wary.

Aphrodite scampers down, hands him his staff with a sweet smile and a twinkle in her eyes.

*She may be a tart, but she's a nice tart...* Hermes is grateful.

Hermes takes a quick shifty round. Po-faced Athena, always the superior moody cow, still preening from her recent besting of Poseidon, lets her smirk do the talking. That smirk, which will endure for millennia until it simply becomes known as wearing a Patel. Silence is how she got her reputation for wisdom; keep schtum and everyone thinks you're clever. But Hermes knows better.

Next to Athena, Artemis scowls, her pretty, top lip curled in an unvoiced snarl. She was clearly still pissed about the dead senator.

*Who cares? She dares not touch me here. Not in front of Dad.*

'Whenever you are ready, Hermes.' Zeus is impatient.

*Cripes, this is big.*

'Yes Sir, ready.'

'Find that lout, Dionysus. Tell him we want him here, immediately.'

Hermes doesn't need telling twice. He begins his lift off.

'I haven't finished.'

Hermes drops like a stone. 'Sorry, Dad.'

Zeus's glare is Gorgons-grade.

*Bugger. Not Dad. Not Dad. Not Dad. Dad is a stickler for protocol.*

'Sorry, Sir.'

'We also want his gang of reprobates. Hypnos, Eros, Priapus and Morpheus, make sure that one leaves his poppies behind.' Zeus looks at his fellow Olympians. 'What do they call themselves?'

'The Liberators,' says Ares resplendent in his gleaming armour. 'As if.'

'One more thing, Hermes,' Zeus says, narrowing his eyes.

*Oh hell, he's heard about the party on Rhodes.*

'No exceptions, no excuses, understood?'

'Understood, Sir.'

'What are you waiting for, boy? Applause?'

'N-no Sir. Yes Sir. Sorry Sir. Right. You've finished? Right, I'm off.' Hermes rises but at speeding-off altitude, he flies in tight right-hand circles, like a demented bee in front of the whole supercilious congregation. The bloody broken wing has knocked his steering alignment out.

It takes an hour to fix, but once done, he's away. Hermes is pump, pump, pumped. An urgent directive from Olympus itself. Head Honcho. Big Daddy. Zeus himself.

He knows where to find Dio. Every year, as the new grapes grow heavy and lush, Dionysus's personal mission is to finish last year's wine before the new harvest. The guy parties methodically north to south. Hermes punches a couple of bumbling pigeons out of his way as he turns south, such is his delight.

At Oinopolis, Hermes finds Dio snoring under a barrel, his mouth positioned to catch the dribs and drabs from the uncorked funnel. Dio's golden diadem of vine leaves is buried in the dust beside him, his tunic sodden with regurgitated wine, his breath rancid.

Hermes toes Dio. Nothing.

'Come on, wake up.' He prods Dio's gelatinous belly with his staff until one of Dio's eyelids unsticks a bleary fraction before squeezing shut again.

'Dio! Dio, come on.'

'Hermes, you piece of goat's crap, Hephaestus' anvil is hammering in my head, and unless you have a very, and I mean very, good reason to be here, I'm going to shove you head first through the plughole of this cask. Three guesses where the bloody cork will go.' His words scritch and squeeze out of his dry lips.

'Zeus wants to see you, like yesterday.'

Dionysus bolts upright and clutches his head.

'Oh shit. Oh shit, my head. Oh shit. What have I done? What does he want? Oh shit.'

'Dunno. But they want you, Morpheus, Hypnos and Eros as well. And what's his name with the big dick...

Priapus?'

Dionysus's eyes, cherry blossom pink without the charm, blink. His tongue, a terminal shade of icterus, swabs his bulbous lips. 'What do you mean *they*?'

'The Twelve.' Hermes twirls Dio's diadem on his foot.

'*All* Twelve? What the hell...give me that, sonny?' Dio grabs his crown and slips it on his head.

'Dio, if I were you...'

'Well, you're not are you, you jumped up carrier pigeon?' Dionysus looks as brittle as he sounds.

Hermes drifts upwards. 'At least I can see straight. Like I say, unless you are tired of being you, you know how vindictive Dad is, I'd have a bath, round up your mates and get over to Olympus PDQ. I'm off, but make sure you're sober before you arrive,' he shouts, disappearing into the glare of the sun beating down on Dionysus cradling his head.

Thirty-six hours it takes. Thirty-six hours calling in and promising favours to locate the boys recovering in their bolt-holes after the summer of parties, booze and sex. Best bender ever, Eros had called it some weeks back. At his age, he wasn't ready to stop partying and left the oldies to wind down. Dio left for one last quiet crack at Oinopolis. Morpheus, after a summer fuelled by his beloved poppies, was time-travelling with goats. Only when his brother, Phobetor, put the fear of the Titans and Ephialtes into him, did he emerge from his drugged stupor. Their Father, Hypnos, an impotent debauchee in his dotage, had tried schmoozing up to his wife Nyx, the Goddess of Night, for a bit of slap-and-tickle a week ago. She was pissed as hell, and not in a happy way. She had drawn him into a deep sleep which he couldn't shake off. As a result, he stumbled, farted and tried to curl up asleep every time he stopped moving. As for Eros, after a love fest with a very pretty band of boys in Ephesus, he could barely walk.

'You'd think his anus never had any wrinkles,' says Priapus, who while exhausted, is undeflated from his own extended orgy.

Thirty-six hours is too long and not enough to get the gang presentable. Sober would take longer and they don't have that much time. Dread urges them into some semblance of order. Dishevelled and hungover, they pitch up at Olympus, wilting under the chorus mask stares of the Twelve who are once more seated on thrones in the shaded portico of the Royal Hall. Only Aphrodite smiles when she spies her son Eros.

'Looks like Medusa's given them the once over,' Dionysus burps *sotto voce* to a still-stoned Morpheus.

Hypnos taking advantage of Priapus's abundant member leans against it, trying to stay upright, fighting to keep his eyes open.

The Gods, tight-lipped and silent, wait for Zeus to begin while the Gang of Five sweat and shuffle in the hot open courtyard at the base of the steps.

'Good of you to join us,' Zeus says.

*Like we had a choice.*

Worried by the sarcasm in His Lordship's voice, Dionysus keeps the snipe behind his teeth, deep in his throat.

Eros, his eyes watering, carefully lowers one cheek to perch on the lower step.

'Who said you could sit?' roars out of Zeus. Eros yelps, scurrying upright. 'And what, by the Heavens, took you so long?'

'Well, Zeus, baby, it wasn't easy, you know,' Morpheus giggles. 'We, uh, we...'

'Shut up, shut up, shut up,' Dionysus hisses.

'Speak when you're spoken to, is that clear?' Zeus says. 'You've been summoned for a serious matter, so listen very carefully.'

In the dutiful silence, Hypnos lets rip a twenty-second fart. Definitely virtuoso. Definitely the opening notes of Pan's much-loved tune, *Glory to the Elysian Heroes*. Shock and awe ripple the silence.

Zeus leans forward on his throne, presses his knuckles against his clenched mouth and looks to his brother, Poseidon.

Poseidon, tired of playing second fiddle to his brother, still humiliated by the city's preference for Athena and her lousy olives, wastes no time. Striding forward, trident in hand poised and ready to smote should the chance arise, this is his moment. He swells with righteousness.

'It is the considered opinion of us all,' he intones with gravity, 'that the state of affairs produced by the combined effects of your unlicensed drunkenness, lechery, laziness, excess, disrespect, poppy pushing, debauchery, carnal...'

'Get on with it.' Zeus closes his eyes with patent exasperation.

'Yes, well you get the picture,' Poseidon says, deliberately blocking Athena's frenzied head-bobbing, first from one side, then the other in her eagerness to be seen.

'My Lord Zeus, this is ridiculous,' Athena says. 'As the Peoples' Choice, surely I—'

'Quiet. My brother speaks.'

'Thank you, Brother. As always, true wisdom.' Poseidon hides a smirk from Zeus but not Athena before turning back to Dionysus and his motley crew. 'The mortals are being led astray by your antics and temptations. They are neglecting homes, work and families. And what is worse and far more important is they are not paying any attention to us. Something needs to be done.' Not being privy to what needs to be done, he finishes with a piercing look at each of the five and sits down.

The reprobates look at each other. Hypnos twigs this is serious but seriously considers whether he really gives a shit. Priapus sags ever so slightly until he is left with a half-mongrel under his cloak. Dionysus and Morpheus are suddenly stone-cold sober. Only Eros, too busy making googly eyes at Narcissus waiting his turn for an audience with the Gods to request a proper mirror instead of the rippling river to look at himself, remains oblivious.

As team leader, Dionysus knows he must respond. Gagging for a drink, even water would be welcome, he licks his parched lips.

'But my Lords and Ladies,' he smiles obsequiously as his mind races seeking wriggle room. 'These very... ah...these very talents, attributes, if you will, were bestowed on us by you. What would you have us do?' He ends with a deep bow and a wide flourish of his arm.

'What's the bow in aid of, idiot?' whispers Morpheus.

Dionysus shrugs. 'It seemed a good idea. Hell, have you any better ideas?'

Zeus stands on the uppermost step and looks down at them.

'You don't need to do anything. Rightly, as you point out, you have been given these...whatever. Once given there's no taking back. So, they need a counter balance.'

The other gods start muttering and nodding behind him.

'Hear, hear.'

'About time.'

'Absolutely.'

'Finally.'

Zeus holds up his hand for silence.

No farts this time.

The five purse their lips, furrow their brows and shoot each other questioning looks. Sobriety returns, sleep departs and lust goes walkabout. Whatever is coming is coming now and they aren't looking forward to it.

Zeus claps his hands.

To everyone's surprise, in walk seven stunning maidens and, to Eros's delight, three handsome strapping lads.

'These are your new assistants. They will introduce themselves. I have given them names which sound odd but trust me, they will take them to eternity and back.' He nods to the newcomers. 'Go ahead.'

One by one, each steps forward to announce his or herself. Some of the terms are gobbledygook but will carry down the ages because the gods are omnipotent and foresee the rise of the barbaric Romans.

'Syphilis.'

'Gonorrhea.'

'Chlamydia.'

'Cachexia.'

'Nausea.'

'Vertigo.'
'Insomnia.'
'Verruca.'
'Hepatitis.'
'Delirium.'

# The Stuffed Minimalist

Roan Ellis-O'Neill

As avenues line up with trees,
and drones drop seeds in Myanmar
and Greta Thunberg sails the Atlantic Ocean with Australian YouTube influencers
and your man carries a coffee flask the size of his head
and I won't ask him about his worryingly high intake of caffeinated products
and Bowie warns me that we only have five years left,
I wonder if we could send the Liberal Democrats to Dignitas.

As the tortoise yearns for the hare's loving care
and the sophomore preceptor whips the students into a shape that stymies curiosity,
repeats "who are they? Don't look at your book. Who are they?"
and Galaxie 500 collaborate, not cover, New Order's "Ceremony" in my headphones
and the staff member for whom I turn on the microphones asks me why I've had a bad
experience here then yaps on about how terrorist attacks in Germany
prevent him from emigrating there,
and he attempts to find common ground in snow-fluttering existence,
raking my mind across the patio doors where he dreams
the dream of peace and harmony where terrorists

die off stage
and the DVD collection stagnates into a passive archive
  because nobody watches DVDs anymore and they only seem to gather dust,
I question why don't they just inject the carbon back into the rocks.

As the Queen abolishes Coronation chicken sandwiches
and British Vogue ask two-hundred-and-seventy-eight questions to Iggy Pop regarding his
  chameleon and choice of brie
and dried cranberries simmer in sauces quadrupling the high-oleic sunflower oil percentage
  among the red-stained paper prompts
and we pour our passions down the oesophagus where the train has arrived
  thirty-two minutes late up the smokestack of my menthol cigarette,
I buy a suitcase and close my inventory.

# Sunday on the Boulevard (with my pet lobster)

Dale Hurst

I'd like to introduce you to a unique pet of mine. A creature with whom I shared many a happy moment. You may think I've gone round the twist when I tell you that I found my life's companion in the form of a lobster.

Cats are aloof and always seem to be scheming, while dogs have their boisterous habits. I don't even care to recall the trouble we had cleaning up after our budgerigar. But keeping a lobster required no lifestyle changes or excess of affection. In fact, mine demonstrated a mutual love of the finer things in life. In particular... a penchant for Montecristo cigars.

Now don't ask me how a lobster smokes – they are not especially loquacious creatures. All I can say is that after his meal of shrimp bisque (not cannibalism, before you ask), he would clamber out of his tank, grab a Montecristo from the case, snip off the end with a claw you'd think was made for the job, and, once I had lighted it for him, would smoke it. You don't get such refinement and elegance with a tabby, a Labrador, or your standard tropical aquarium fish!

Of course, taking him out in public turned a few heads. With twice as many smokers in the house now, we were going through the Montecristos in half the time. And Monsieur le Verrier, our local tobacconist, was almost appalled to find a crustacean in his shop.

'Monsieur François!' I remember he cried, '*Qu'est-ce que c'est*? A lobster on your shoulder!'

'You were expecting a parrot? A giant squid? A girl from the *Folies Bergère*? Or perhaps even Humphrey Bogart himself?'

Poor Monsieur le Verrier – too often have I seen his face scrunch up like a bewildered little prune with a shoe brush under its nose to serve as a moustache. Ever since I have been a customer at his very accommodating, if shabby, little shop, I have always held the opinion that he is a man quite pitiful. A dilapidated mole of a man who seems so exhausted by life that he remains deliberately ignorant of all around him for the sake of some peace. It's difficult not to take the tiniest sadistic pleasure in his inability to tell whether I'm being serious or not.

'You are in here sooner than usual, Monsieur,' he declared, still frowning almost fearfully at the bluish-black shellfish clicking its claws atop my coat. 'We did not expect you for another fortnight."

'Another mouth to feed, you see, Monsieur le Verrier, so I will require a double-order of Montecristos this time *s'il vous plaît*.'

Monsieur le Verrier looked close to bursting into tears when he gleaned that I was talking about my pet lobster.

'But, Monsieur—' he began. 'The lobster? Surely it can't—'

'And why on earth not?'

I placed my money on his counter to demonstrate how insistent I was.

'Very well,' the befuddled little tobacconist gave in. '*Vingt-huit de la Montecristo. Cinquante francs, s'il vous plaît.*'

I gave him seventy, a tip for his trouble. After all, how many tobacconists go through their lives selling cigars to lobsters? They surely don't learn that in the training! My lobster snapped his claws again, I assumed with great joy and readiness to break in his new box of Montecristos.

'Monsieur François, a moment more of your time.' Monsieur le Verrier beckoned me closer. 'I have just recalled a piece of information my brother told me once about keeping lobsters.'

'Ah yes, of course – Monsieur Jacques le Verrier from the zoo!' I recollected the man in question – an eminent and esteemed expert in his field – at once. 'Well what is this advice?'

'That lobsters are prone to coughing. But if you feed it an asparagus, it should go away.'

'What excellent advice!' I revelled with glee. 'There will be plenty of coughing to come if he likes these cigars so much!'

'Plenty of asparagus too, in that case.' Monsieur le Verrier was still looking most unsure about the lobster on my shoulder. 'He may not like it at first, but just shove it in and, sooner or later, he will take it. Like you're stuffing a duck for foie gras.'

'You are most kind, Monsieur!' I said, 'And you must pass on my regards to your brother!'

'Oh, I would, but I cannot.'

'Why ever not?'

'He slipped and fell into the shark tank at the zoo,

with a bleeding toe. It was a feeding frenzy within seconds.'

'*Mon Dieu*!' I gasped. '*Quelle dommage*! The secret is sticking with smaller creatures – they present far fewer dangers!'

The lobster snipped at my earlobe with his claw – evidently getting impatient. Just chomping at the bit for a Montecristo.

'Well, *merci beaucoup*, Monsieur le Verrier,' I hastily conceded. 'I'll be back in two weeks.'

It was such a glorious Sunday, I decided to take my companion out to dinner at *Chez l'Armoire* right off the *Boulevard Sainte Lourdes de Biarritz*. The incomparable views of the glistening, crystal sea can only be got from an al fresco seat on the veranda of this top-class restaurant. But like poor Monsieur le Verrier, I fear the hostess did not quite understand my pet. She looked absolutely horrified when she came to take our order and, to my dismay, went to confiscate my lobster.

'*Excusez-moi*!' I protested. 'What do you think you are doing? This is a pet-friendly restaurant!'

'But Monsieur!' replied the hostess. 'The lobster – she is not cooked!'

'*He* is here to eat!'

'Pardon?' the hostess' voice reduced almost to a whimper; she was so confused.

'This is dinner for two, *mademoiselle*! And the lobster will have shrimp bisque to start, with an asparagus salad to follow.'

At the mention of asparagus, the lobster began to splutter, which quite frankly scared the hostess out of her skin. I could not blame her in actual fact. The sound of a lobster coughing is quite extraordinary – not the sort of thing one could predict. Like a cat trying to hack up a hairball while having its head stuffed rather unceremoniously into a paper bag at the same time. A crackly and snappy kind of retching.

'On second thought,' I piped up. 'Bring the asparagus first, and the bisque for afters. And perhaps a little caviar? Wait a minute – do you want the cocktail menu, or shall we share a bottle of champagne?' I directed the question to the lobster, who quite frankly did not look too fussed one way or the other – as long as the much-needed asparagus arrived first.

'All right! All right! The champagne then! A bottle of the Pierre Beauvais, *s'il vous plaît,*' I silkily requested from the hostess.

Off she went, shaking her head every few steps as though this was the oddest thing she had ever seen. In her line of work, surely not! All sorts of people and pets must come through the doors of Chez l'Armoire! I heard of the Comtesse de Montreuil bringing her pelican for a lunch with her friends, and the actress Ingrid Oberfeldt made the headlines by holding a birthday party for the family's beloved tarantula. My lobster – his unprecedented predilection for smoking notwithstanding – was surely quite mundane by comparison.

The asparagus salad was brought soon after and placed down in front of the lobster. The hostess did not linger to observe, which in truth was probably for the best. It made for rather chaotic work, trying to feed a lobster a stalked vegetable. Its mouth did not seem big enough to eat it, but Monsieur le Verrier's advice rang in my head: 'Just shove it in and, sooner or later, he will take it.'

And eventually, he did. But the added exercise of consuming the thing made us both in the mood for a cigar, which we indulged in as our main courses came out – my duck roasted with olives and caviar, and the lobster's sumptuous bisque.

There was no time for dessert, for after his dinner, the lobster began to cough again. So, smuggling out the remaining asparagus, I took him for some fresh air along the boulevard, turning the heads of many a passerby as we did so. The lobster hardly seemed interested in the asparagus, for all his spluttering. He seemed as tempted as I to just dive into that flawless sea water. But I was hardly dressed for the occasion, and he could not possibly go in coughing all over the place. Once more, I stuffed a green stalk down him.

The coughing did stop eventually, but I came to suspect it was not the asparagus that did the trick. Because my lobster died while on the Boulevard Sainte Lourdes de Biarritz. The story you have just heard is the same one I told Monsieur le Verrier the following day, when I went to confront him rather indignantly about his late brother's ultimately dubious advice.

'You told me that the coughing would go away if I force-fed the lobster asparagus!' I quite rightly told him. 'What do you have to say for yourself?'

'Well Monsieur, you may have done that part, but you missed one rather vital step in looking after a lobster!'

'Do you think it was the cigars that killed him?' I asked.

'I highly doubt they helped matters, but there's

something even more basic that he should have had.'

'What's that?'

'Well, he was a lobster, Monsieur. You should have kept him in some water!'

# Don't Know What to Say

Helen Ribchester

I don't know what to say
when I'm worried about you.
There is no book of words
that will tell me what to do.

I know you're hurting so,
in every kind of way,
but I don't know how to help you
when I don't know what to say.

Just call and ask me how I am
or text me for a natter.
It's contact I appreciate,
the content doesn't matter.

I have this thing called cancer,
it's a nasty little git.
It's taking stuff away from me,
and it's mangled my left tit.

This cancer is a scary thing,
it will take a while to mend,
and while I'm on this journey
I'm going to really need my friends.

Don't hide yourself away from me
not knowing what to say.
Be normal, chat and laugh with me,

it's best for all of us that way.

Invite yourself for coffee,
take me shopping, make me tea.
Don't wait for me to shout for help,
you know that's just not me.

Make fun of me, that's normal,
Call me names, like Uncle Fester.
Don't go all soft and soppy,
And whatever you do, don't pester.

Then when it's done, that's over,
We need to get back where we were.
Yes, it's part of me, will always be,
But in time it'll be a vague blur.

So treat me normal now, my friend,
Don't pussy foot around.
I'm no warrior, and no victim,
And this thing won't take me down.

# Scuttled

Martin Costello

*for the Arc of Bonesea, a Far Country*

eye / ahy / ‘aɪ /
[27] Nautical.
the precise direction from which a wind is blowing

‘I recall the time I was run over by a fast-moving story at a narrative intersection,’ said the old sailor, rocking his chair on the porch overlooking the harbour, the wailing child in his lap seeking consolation. The little boy had been in a collision with his sister, his knee was bruised and there were grazes, of course, to his pride. The old man, who had a mariner’s tale for every occasion - though few that anyone understood - sought to soothe away the hurt by stroking his hair and recounting the time he received wounds to his own vanity, many years ago, one hundred nautical miles off the coast of Grand Barbarie. Whether the telling eased the discomfort of his grandson does not enter this story, since the boy himself is but a device.

***

No-one knows precisely what story is upon them until it breaks on the shore of time and circumstance, and is recounted later through the diffusing lenses of perspective, context, hindsight, style and intention. If we knew the story into which we dived, to swim like a sleek cod in ocean streams of warm agency, cold coincidence and buoyant tropical determinism, and could see the outcome in all its complex causal glory, we probably wouldn't even get changed into our narrative trunks. We'd stay at home, in the warm and dry, and get fat on the never-changing surety of life-without-incident.

Thus it is for the *Purple Bruise* and all who sail in her, as she cleaves out of the dock on Wharfside, into Coffin Harbour, away from Spittal Bay and out into the Wide Ocean under the steady hand of Captain Asa Liechtenstein and his crew of able seamen, that they know not precisely what is to become of them for the sake of a cracking yarn. Powered by improbable engines the extra-rapid barque is on its way to misty Antediluvia, or somesuch farther shore, and though every good Bonesman - and woman, and person of indeterminate or undeclared gender - knows that they are always pitching into the eye of a potential narrative storm, they can't really see much past their own nose or into the heart of the story, so they will metaphorically shrug their shoulders dismissively and just get on with it.

'Fire up the improbable engines, Mr. McCracken,' says the Captain, over the ship intercom to his chief engineer, once the barque is healthily beyond the bells of Dogside which mark the audible range of the chill Bonesea shore. They have departed on the early tides and there should be no need to engage the even-more-improbable Fluid Time gyros on this journey, which is a good thing so far as the crew of the *Purple Bruise* are concerned. Nobody wants to be pitched into the middle of next week unnecessarily.

Here is the First Mate Collarbone Kildare, who

was once a licensed mariner on the ill-fated barque the *Overproof*; and so too the watchman Paddack Hildebrand, and the sonar operator Elid Sampson. Here is the master helmsman Jim Moon, as old as wives' tales, whose real name is Uimi Munuku, a prodigious tea-drinker; and Paracelsus McCracken the Ship's Engineer who has care of the engines as well as the ship's terrier, the old sea dog Cully: and a fine Bonesea Terrier she is too. Here is the meteorologist and radar operator Cleve Smayling who sees all the weather, and the Commsman Corfe Tonge who hears all the chatter. Here is the deckhand Brat Warst, a Sachsen by birth who turned his back on the landed lubbers to enlist with the Bonesfolk. And here are some additional seamen, able bodies all, ready at a moment's notice to step in and have minor incidents of plot emptied upon them for the good of the narrative: Ogden Yellowhammer and Brón Ruggles, late of the *Custom of The Sea*, steady men of minor tales past; Scaddon Porthollow, Bud Gole, and the brothers Boswarva and Godolphin Stave of whom you had not heard, before today. Thank you mariners of the *Purple Bruise*! Thank you for what you have done and what you will do in furtherance of the Arc of that Far Country of Bonesea, the story of an ocean-faring country, though you cannot possibly know what is ahead.

'Storm ahead, Captain! Radar is warning of a narrative tailwind coming in from the direction Sinister-by-Sinister-Occidental,' says Mr. Smayling.

'Whatever next?' wonders the Captain, out loud. One hundred miles off the Barbary Coast is no place to be overtaken by a narrative tailwind, which is sure to push the vessel into some kind of unwelcome story that the Captain, the crew, and The Passengers could really rather do without. Mr. Smayling provides a number of meteorological and narrative data points, suggesting the storm will overtake them within the next twenty lines or so, and is of a degree that might best be termed 'quite ferocious'.

'Shinbones!' swears the Captain, using the third worst expletive in the Boney Linga, 'prepare for an early plot twist, lads!' and then adds, with all due and proper consideration, 'and lasses, and persons of indeterminate or undeclared gender!'

The First Mate looks out from the bridge to the Sinister directions. All seems calm enough, to the naked eye, except... there! And... there! And there... and there and there! 'Codwall, Captain!' says Collarbone. A wave of millions of Enness Cod rise out of the sea, thrashing and writhing into the air to a height of twenty metres or more.

'Prepare to be codwalloped!' orders the Captain via ship's intercom. 'Mr. Moon, turn us into that wave, I will not be pushed headlong into a new scene without a fight!'

The prodigious tea-drinker and helmsman prepares to turn the ship about, but before the codwall is even close, there begins a great rattling noise rather like hail, and the sky dims as the *Purple Bruise* is deluged.

'It's raining pens!' radios the able seaman Paddack Hildebrand, who is up on the watch.

'Shattered pelvis!' swears the Captain, using the second worst expletive in the Boney Linga, for he knows a metaphoric omen when he sees one, 'brace yourselves!'

The codwall up out of the Sinister-by-Sinister-

Occidental hits the *Purple Bruise* at three-quarters to fore-on. The bounty of the sea is smeared all over the deck in a bloody mess of mangled cod and associated trophobiotic organisms; a quagmire of pinks, reds and silvers mixing slowly with the spilled black and blue inks of a million ball pens that fell on the ship ahead of the narrative storm front. The engine stalls.

There is a buzz on the intercom from the Ship's Engineer. 'Engine's stalled, Captain,' he says, 'looks like that tailwind has thrown a syntagma in the works.'

The Captain barely has time to wonder what in the name of - when the radar operator Mr. Smayling pipes up again. 'Sorry to bother you Captain, but we have incoming on the radar. Small launch, coming from Septenward.'

The Captain uses the worst expletive in the Boney Linga.

'Message from the launch, Captain,' says Comms Officer Tonge, 'it's Messrs. Couth and Ruly, Sir - the Narrative Agents.'

The Captain uses the worst expletive in the Boney Linga again.

The ship's terrier, Cully, also has news. She barks urgently at the Captain. Paracelsus McCracken radios over the intercom. 'She says we've entered uncharted narrative waters,' crackles McCracken, him having a good understanding of Cully's complex lexicon, 'and we might want to think about dropping the lifeboats.'

The Captain uses the worst expletive in the Boney Linga for the third time, and then apologises to the ship's terrier. 'Excuse my Spanish,' he says, regaining his composure.

***

'I still don't see why we must scuttle the boat,' says Captain Liechtenstein, standing in one of the *Purple Bruise* lifeboats, his crew about him, and some already down in the water on other lifeboats.

The Narrative Agents Messrs. Couth & Ruly are the last men standing on the deck of the Bonesea barque, not six months built in the yard at Spittalsea, a fine specimen of the nuclear- and fluid time-powered vessels unmatched across the Wide Enness Ocean and beyond.

'My engineer Mr. McCracken - a fine engineer, Sirs - says the improbable engines can be up and running again in two days,' continues the Captain, 'and we'll have this gore off the decks in a couple hours with some industrial bleach and a good shanty. It seems highly improbable to me that we'd sink the ship on account of that, gentlemen. And your appearing here out of the blue is not only highly suspicious but barely credible, in the grand scheme of things,' - Captain Liechtenstein is hardly impressed to be losing his new ship already.

'All for the good of the narrative, Captain,' calls back Mr. Couth, the sinister agent with the chipper Received English accent, twirled mustachios, finest civilian woolens and silk threads, and murderous dead eyes.

'Narrative my tibia,' decries the Captain dismissively, 'who'll believe this contrived nonsense?'

'No-one will remember by the end of chapter eight,' says Mr. Ruly, another chipper fellow with mustaches and a ruinous look in his dead eyes -

' - chapter four, more likely,' interjects Mr. Couth -

'...and we are playing the long story,' continues Mr. Ruly: 'we want this fine machine at the bottom of the ocean, Captain Liechtenstein - perhaps you have eyes only for the moment, and cannot see the intersection of another plot, right here, right now, but thirty fathoms deeper down?'

'Now just a minute, do you mean to say I'm losing my ship to a narrative plant?'

'Call it an investment in the Arc of Bonesea,' says Mr. Couth, as the *Purple Bruise* lists to starboard.

# LOVE

# Home Home

## Niamh Donnellan

Ciara could feel spring in the air as she drove home. The fields by the motorway unspooled a flickering tape of lambs playing on fresh green grass, cattle raising their heads to the sky after a long winter indoors, and juddering tractors ploughing the waking earth. Luke snored gently in his car seat, lulled to sleep by the sound of the radio and the warm sun. Ciara's phone rang and she tapped the dashboard quickly so as not to wake him. Her sister's voice came through, breathless.

'Where are you?'

'Nearly home. I'm going to do a spring clean.'

'Great, I'll call over in twenty minutes, I'm out for a walk.'

'No, not Dublin. I meant home home.'

'Offaly? You drove all the way there this morning?'

'Yes. Someone needs to keep an eye on the place.'

'Someone needs to sell the place. It's been two years.'

'Someone.'

'Yeah. Someone.'

She could hear her sister smile.

'Fine. Enjoy the day out. Say hello to the old place for me.'

'Will do.'

Two years, had it really been that long? Ever since her mother died, their family home had lain empty. At first the freshness of grief stopped them from thinking about what to do next. When her brother finally broached the subject the following Christmas, gently suggesting that they sell the house and split the profit, she surprised herself with the strength of her reaction. No. It was still too soon. How about keeping it as a summer home for the three families? Somewhere to create happy childhood memories for the next generation. The others had scrunched up their faces. The house was a 1970's bungalow in the middle of nowhere, not a picturesque seaside cottage. Dragging the kids there had been hard enough when it involved a visit to Granny and Grandad. Without them, it was just a cold, dark building with no internet. But it was Christmas Day, they'd all had a few drinks, best to leave it.

Another year went by. The house remained empty and her dreams of sunny family holidays hadn't come to pass. Her brother was in Australia and her sister had never found the time. To be fair, her own family weren't overly keen either. The first time they went down was Easter and the kids complained of the cold. So, they waited until the height of summer to go again and were eaten alive by midges. The following year John had insisted on two weeks in France. Then it was Autumn, back to school and the weekend routines of football matches and swimming lessons, Halloween parties, snowy December roads, icy January roads, St. Patrick's Day parades, and before she knew it, the days were getting longer again and nobody had been down home in months.

She turned left onto the familiar road past a copse of trees at the edge of their field, and then the old house was in sight. There it was, unchanged, sitting back from the road down a narrow potholed lane lined with nodding daffodils. The hedgerows were alive with little songbirds who flew and perched, flew and perched, just ahead of the car as if leading her on. Smoke curled out lazily from the chimney.

It took her a minute to register the activity. Weird. She'd just spoken to her sister, who else could be there? Maybe a neighbour had come to check the place? Paddy down the road was well known for taking matters into his own hands. Mam had been convinced he had binoculars to watch the comings and goings of the neighbours. She would bet money he still had a spare key for 'emergencies', the word having quite a loose definition in his books. She pulled up to the house and hopped out of the car. Bloody cheek of the man. She hauled a sleepy Luke from his car seat and marched up to the back door. Just as she suspected, it wasn't locked. She flung it open.

A man stood bent over the kitchen table, his back to her. Not Paddy. This man was around her age, dark hair, dark skin. Ciara let out a scream at the intruder. The man turned around at the unexpected sound, revealing a small girl around Luke's age sitting at the table, drawing with crayons. The little girl looked up at Ciara with big brown eyes, assessed the threat as minimal and went back to her drawing. Ciara frowned. This didn't look like a burglary.

'What are you doing here?'

The man looked more worried than aggressive.

'I live here.'

'No you don't. This is my house.'

'You are Maureen?'

'No. That's my mother. Was my mother. It's my mother's house. My family home. How do you know

Mam?'

'There is still some post coming. I keep it there.'

He pointed to a neat pile of letters and leaflets on the counter.

'So, who are you? A squatter?'

'I am Abdullah. This is my daughter Lena. I am sorry, my English, squatter?'

'Oh, for Christ's sake. You are here without permission ... illegally ... not allowed ... criminal..."

'Yes. I apologise.' He bowed his head.

'Right. Well. That's not good enough.'

'Yes, of course.'

They stood in silence. A loud snap made Ciara jump. The toaster had popped. Lena tugged on her father's sleeve. Abdullah shrugged at Ciara in the universal language of 'kids, what can you do?' Ciara watched as he buttered the toast and cut it into little triangles before placing the plate in front of his daughter. Luke took the chance to wiggle out of her arms. He climbed onto a chair and began eating the toast alongside Lena. Ciara felt her head start to spin and, stumbling slightly, she sat down heavily on Dad's armchair by the stove.

Abdullah looked concerned.

'Can I offer you tea? For the shock?'

'Em, yes ok.'

He filled the kettle and took two mugs from the draining board, spoons from the drawer and tea bags from the press. It was the practised routine of a man at home in his own kitchen. It set her teeth on edge. He handed her a mug of pale, yellow liquid.

'It's *zouhourat*, made from hibiscus flowers, calming.'

She took a small sip. It tasted sweet and flowery.

The warm sound of daytime radio chatted in the background. Abdullah sat at the kitchen table staring at the mug of tea in front of him.

She felt the blood return to her face and her anger flared again in the face of his serenity.

'So why did you think it was ok to break into somebody else's home?'

He leaned forward slightly and began to speak.

'I came to Ireland from Syria three years ago. We decided to leave when my wife became pregnant. A fresh start, you know. We reached a refugee camp in Turkey. Unfortunately ...'

He glanced at Lena.

'Unfortunately, my wife did not survive the birth.'

He gulped down some tea.

'I continued on to Ireland. I was told that we would be placed temporarily in a direct provision centre while my application was processed. But it is taking much longer than I expected. I cannot work until my case is heard. I thought why not improve my English, so I volunteered at a charity shop a few days a week. A nice Nigerian lady looked after Lena while I worked. I took the bus to Tullamore and that is when this all began.'

'When what began?' Ciara asked impatiently. She hadn't asked for his life story, no matter how harrowing.

'I stared out the bus window for two months at this empty house. I imagined living here, Lena playing in the garden. Finally, one day I got off the bus and walked down the lane, looking in the windows at the dusty rooms. I waited one more month. I did not want to be this person who steals a home, a squinter?'

'Squatter.'

'Yes, I did not want to be this person so I waited and dreamed. But I decided on Lena's third birthday I could not face another year of my little bird living in a cage. My friend has a phrase: "better to ask forgiveness than permission".'

Ciara huffed.

'So, I packed our bag and we took the bus in the rain to the house. Oh, Lena thought it was such an adventure.'

He smiled at Ciara as a fellow parent and then seemed to catch himself. He sat up straighter.

'I never took it for granted, I assure you. I made repairs, worked in the garden, planted vegetables.' He tapped the table to bullet point his productivity. 'I have a list of work I will do around the house.'

He pointed to the fridge where there was indeed a long list pinned amongst Lena's crayon drawings.

'I am truly sorry. For me, I would stay in direct provision, but for Lena ... I had to take this chance. Even these few months have been good for her. To play in the garden. To have her own room. I would like to stay here *in sha allah*, god willing. Maybe we could make an arrangement ... but I understand this is your home. I have no right.'

With that he trailed off. His face that had become animated lapsed back into resignation as he waited for another nameless Irish person to decide his fate.

Ciara's breathing had slowed as he talked. At first, she barely heard what he said, anger drumming in her ears. But gradually his quiet voice and the warm kitchen took their effect. She looked around. He had kept the place well - even, truth be told, improved upon it. The kitchen was neat as a pin. The sink was polished to a high sheen and it looked like he had repaired the leaky tap. There was a vase of flowers on the windowsill, daffodils from the garden mixed with some greenery from the hedge. Mam always did it that way too. She hadn't seen the house this clean and cosy in years. His story too sounded plausible. It chimed with all those news articles and opinion pieces in the papers lamenting the fate of asylum seekers in Ireland. She had read them in sympathy and indignation, and had signed the petitions.

She paused before speaking, trying to reflect his measured calm.

'Well you can't stay here.'

'Of course, I understand.'

She had been prepared for an argument.

'I mean, I know it's empty most of the year but it's not that simple. It's our family home.'

He nodded and looked slightly to her left out the window to the garden where the sound of the birds drifted in on a cool spring breeze.

'We will leave as soon as possible. Is Saturday ok? I will need to make arrangements.'

Ciara was discommoded by his immediate acceptance of his fate. It softened her.

'I can give you until the end of the month.'

'That's very generous.'

She was put out. She was the one in the right here but this calm man made her feel like he was being the reasonable one, squatting in her home for months now.

'Right. Well, I suppose that's everything.'

'Thank you.'

'You're welcome.'

He walked her to the door. He was still acting like it was his house. She could feel her irritation rising again.

'Luke, get in the car.'

He trailed across, scuffing his shoes in the gravel.

'Mam, I don't want to go home. I want to stay here. I want to play with Lena.'

He squirmed and whined as she wrestled him into his car seat.

As she drove down the lane, she looked in the rear view mirror. Lena stood at the door waving goodbye to Luke. Abdullah stood behind her, his hand resting gently on her brown curls. It was a gesture she remembered from her own father.

Oh, fuck it. She began to reverse the car back up the lane. There was an arrangement to be made.

# The McCallum Chin

Sharon Black

Protruding, almost petulant, this chin
runs through the women of our bloodline

like a rhizome, sprouting its potato
through the pale soil

of our Ayrshire faces. These chins
don't quiver, dimple, or itch to fight:

they're unassuming all their lives
then jut, spectacular, above an ageing neck.

There's Grandma Roberts in her housecoat,
a tuft of wiry hairs on hers;

Gran, all flowery plates and fruitcake slices,
under hers two loops of pearls;

Mum, buttoned up, heading for the leisure club,
hers shiny from Olay. And mine,

one in a queue stretching across the generations –
deceased, alive, and waiting to be born –

bobbing up the line, waggling
at the family gossip, stepping forward

when our names are called, rising briefly into view

then out again, making babies,

getting jobs, falling ill,
burying our dead,

doing our best to take it on our chins,
doing our best to keep them up.

# Taxidermy

Anna Seidel

A silver crystal owl scent bottle burst
on her day of death, unearthing the ground.
Bearing a bounty of hidden treasures,
each subtly enveloping a story
of life's ephemeral nature.
The scent of leather flower settles
in a near century-old bowl,
still marked by the shining drool
of rattling stray dog teeth, she'd fed,
while listening for a rhythm,
in their abandoned souls' screaming.
Perfume spills on the typewriter she used,
to build, bit by bit, the advance obituaries
of dotty dictators with.
Duck decoys on her desk still hold notes
pulled from her marvellous, magpie mind,
cluttered with all sorts of useless information.
She knew
the colour in a pitch-black room was "eigengrau".
She knew
cats couldn't taste sweets due to a genetic defect.
She knew
apple seeds contained cyanide.
Folded over the back of her chair still
"The Art of French Cooking" rests,
opened on "Tarte Tatin",
holding the secret of at least four lovers
encrypted in pencilled ingredient lists.

Memories continued in silence,
sawdust fillers to curious dioramas
that kept those we love alive.

# Big Adventure at Boulder Creek

## Bill Richardson

*for Colin*

Dante aimed for what he called excessive beauty
and according to Augustine,
what God wanted was excessive love,
but when we went exploring Boulder Creek together,
son,
that green shirt I wore was plain and ugly
as was your navy football top,
and yet this photo shows we got on fine.
I pulled the shirt out last night to discard it:
after twenty years it wants to know
if you and I still smile to be together.
No one can mend those frays around the collar
and nothing lasts forever, I reply.
Old and tired the shirt is looking now
though in this picture still it's in its prime,
but in the photo too there's something stunning,
ingrained enough to never go away.

# Churchill Street

## Tim Relf

Clearing out a loft – a box a file a packet of photos
then there you are.
It's the second year and you're in my flat
smiling.
Would 'self-conscious' be the way to describe how you
look (I suppose having your photo
  taken was more of a thing back then)?
Were you embarrassed? Amused? Happy? Or were
you bored? With standing around? With
          me and that flippin' camera?
With me? It's as if
you had something to tell me,
perhaps were even on the brink of so doing –
I don't remember. I do remember
how your smile, then as now, had floored me leaving
the photo place (was it a Boots?) on that faraway high
street
so instead
I concentrate on the red scarf, the puffa jacket, the
earrings (did I buy you those?)
and slightly out of shot: the saggy sofa, the Smiths
poster, the cellophane-covered windows
then splitting up (I still can't recall exactly why we
did) and graduating
and you emigrating
and hearing you'd had a son
later, a daughter too.

But what if it was something else altogether, that look?
What if it was, say, love?
Love – set silently in your expression;
your smile, screaming it.
Yes. What if that's it – love?
Right here,
right there –
caught in the corner of a cold house,
pressed into this packet,
among these people who became people
I don't know?

# Dying Embers

Nikki Nova

His words – dying embers.
I think he was telling me a story
but all I heard was poems.
Every rhyme from the tip of his lips
is carved in my bones.
And his name... oh his name!
I can't release it from my grip.
There are fragments of him,
like shrapnel embedded in my skin.

This world... he doesn't understand.
It seems somewhat quieter with him.
I've never known anyone
wear the moonlight quite like him.
Sitting here on that pier,
I cannot help but wonder – can he ever be whole?
How many oceans it would take?
But we can create the new in the ruins of the old.
Only with the sand between our toes.

# My Love, My Violin

Martyn Smiles

O dolce, dolce, My Love,
let us play a little longer,
con expressione, con brio,
sometimes allegro
- ah allegro, allegro assai!
Sometimes far more slow.
You might say lento, largo.
No, no! Rather: adagio.

O dolce, dolce, My Love, with you
I'm animato and appassionato.
Let me hold you again fermato, feroce
and hold you messa di voce,
until your neck and breasts
are ben marcato,
or, as some might note
- though I hope none know -
in a pattern most bizzaro.

O My Love, My Violin,
in the right hands
you are a lover above all others.
But in the grip of some just a poor drum,
while others still can only scratch out a screech
- each convinced he is The Maestro.

Love, Rapture Divine,
is mine –all Mine!-
with the ease of a glissando,
when you are in my arms
and my heart is played pizzicato.
You hear my heart's tone
grow louder each and every day
until... eventually?
No, not finale,
but da capo.

# A glossary of terms

*dolce* - sweet
*con expressione* - with feeling
*con brio* - lively
*allegro assai* - very fast
*lento* - slowly
*largo* - broadly
*adagio* - at a slow tempo
*animato* - animated
*appassionato* - deeply emotional
*fermato* - prolonged
*feroce* - fiercely
*messa di voce* - a sustaining a note while increasing the volume
*ben marcato* - strongly
*bizarro* - bizarre
*glissando* - a continuous sliding between notes
*pizzicato* - the plucking of a string
*da capo* - from the beginning

# The Boy on the Bike

## Henry Tydeman

The day after Nan died, Charlie started cycling.

When she was in the hospital - he hadn't visited her, the prospect terrified him - he'd wandered about the house without anything to do, unable to relax, troubled by a strange, nervous sadness. He'd been nervous before, on school sports days, and sad (films sometimes made him cry when no one was looking) but never this unsettling combination that made his heart beat fast and his mind ache. He couldn't concentrate on anything else. He'd pick up a book or turn on the television, but within minutes they'd just seem like unwanted distractions. And he wasn't hungry; the sandwiches Dad made were left untouched, forlorn.

He knew that she was dying. His parents had said so. She'd fallen over in her house and banged her head. He would listen to Dad talking on the phone and could tell straight away that he was speaking to Mum because it was his serious voice. There were long gaps when Dad hardly spoke. Charlie would sit in the next room and hear the call end and his father's purposeful footsteps. 'She's sleeping,' he'd say, or 'She's the same as before.' Then, five days after she fell, the footsteps were a little slower and he knew immediately.

'Nan died this morning, Charlie.'

The bike was in the shed. He wheeled it out and stood with it on the pavement in the still air and the quiet. He was surprised at one thing. His feelings hadn't changed since he'd found out. He had expected that an ocean of tears would pour forth like it did in films, that he would cling to his parents, shaking, gasping amidst the flood, but that at least the nervousness would subside. But none of this was right; he hadn't cried and the nerves remained, prickling. What was there to be nervous about now? The bike was another attempt to take his mind off things. He didn't hold out much hope. He'd never cycled on the road before, and so he decided to stick to the pavements. He wouldn't go far, just around the block or along a couple of streets and back. The sky was white and indifferent and hung above like an old sheet or a cheaply painted ceiling.

Charlie sat on the seat, gripped the handlebars, and carefully started pedalling. He wobbled, but quickly rebalanced, each of the muscles in his arms and legs doing exactly as they should, as if they had minds of their own, working together like a troupe of dancers in a musical, the end result a fabulous display of human ingenuity, and he was away, chugging over paving stones, negotiating cracks and little bumps here and there. It felt... good, *bracing*, the way it engaged the whole body, an all-encompassing activity, the arms and legs and chest which had been weighed down and deadened by unremitting, crude *feeling* for days were now in motion again, and he felt lighter and went faster. The crisp air on his face burrowed in wherever it could, and he opened his eyes wider - and even his mouth - as he went along. It seemed to revive him. His clogged mind was a little clearer, and he felt a kind of... calm.

So, he went out on the bike every day, and when he

did it always seemed that the sadness and the nerves were somehow crowded out, and he stopped noticing them. He started going for longer, and further, wheeling the bike carefully across the roads so he could try new streets, different blocks. Neighbours were cheered by the pleasant, innocent sight of the boy on the bike (though some scowled and felt that cycling should never be allowed on the pavements).

Nan's house was only four streets away. He'd avoided it for the first week, but then, on a damp Monday morning, he found himself there at its end and paused. He thought that it was somehow childish of him to miss out this street deliberately, and so, feeling brave, he turned and began pedalling along the pavement. He was thinking of her as he came up alongside the house. The curtains were closed. There was no light beyond them. The place looked so lonely, like a lost dog, tired of whimpering but still plagued by fear and emptiness. Charlie felt a rush of vivid emotion in his cheeks and behind his eyes, and quickly - before the tears that he knew were coming - he set off again. All evening, he thought of the house, with its blue door and the darkness behind the curtains. He didn't tell Dad, and he realised that as well as the sadness, he felt so *sorry* for Nan. The same way he felt at school when someone was being picked on. But at school you could say something, or the person could fight back, stick up for themselves; there was a way out, the potential for justice, or consolation at least. It wasn't the same for her.

And yet, he kept on coming back, standing in the same spot and thinking the same things. He remembered all the different rooms, and every time he did, she was there, sat on the sofa or stood up chopping vegetables in the kitchen. Then he'd make himself picture them empty, dust on the surfaces, complete silence. Perhaps there was a half-finished plate of something. And the pity he felt grew, because she'd been unfairly treated - that's how it seemed. Taken away like that, all of a sudden and without warning, halfway through breakfast. It wasn't right. At home he hugged the pillow and imagined it was her. He'd stand outside her place every day and feel the surge coming on, waves of feeling, and yet after a while he could also tell - though he would never have admitted this to anyone - that he was somehow... *enjoying* it. It was a strange thing. He'd started going out on the bike to get away from all that - and it had worked - yet now he almost craved it, he sought it out, the deep ache, the profusion of feelings, the inevitable tears. There was something about it that he needed, that he went back for. It seemed to satisfy him.

He was standing in the usual spot, the sad house ahead of him, his bike off to one side (he'd started leaning it against a lamppost). He gazed at the bricks, at the windows, at all of it, and the feelings came on as strong as ever. He was basking in them, like a reptile in the sunlight, in the misery he had found that was his own and no one else's, and for a split second he thought that the sun had flashed against the kitchen window. But it hadn't, and Charlie felt his insides suddenly drop away. The light in the kitchen had been turned on. He could see clearly, behind the blinds, strips of yellow. Signs of life.

Charlie was scared. He looked around in the empty street then back up towards the kitchen. The light shone. A burglar. It *had* to be a burglar. That thought made him angry. It was an outrage! He knew the sensible thing would be to go home and tell Dad, but something drove him on, he hardly stopped to think at all, and up he went to the front door and pushed against it. It was unlocked. He stood on the little porch and listened. Yes, there was definitely someone in the kitchen. He heard the clanging of plates, footsteps and ... music. They'd put the radio on! He imagined it was a group of them, and that they were dancing in celebration as they filled their bags with Nan's old cutlery and whatever else took their fancy. Fear and rage mingled inside him. He wanted to run, but he'd never forgive himself if he did. He had to stand face to face with them, for Nan's sake. It was the least he could do. He hoped they'd take one look at him and scarper, and he could say that he'd frightened them off. She'd be so proud.

He crept round the corner and saw where the light from the kitchen spilled out onto the carpet in the hallway. The music was louder. There were no voices. His heart was beating so very fast. He'd already decided to show himself, to shout, or scream, or go for them perhaps, with his fists. He was a foot from the open door. He took a deep breath, tensed, and stepped defiantly into the light, so they could see him, and he opened his mouth to cry out, as loudly as he could.

Nan gasped. Then smiled.

'Oh, it's you.'

Charlie's mouth stayed open. There she was, with her apron on, a big serving spoon in her hand.

'It's shepherd's pie, I know you like shepherd's pie.'

It really was shepherd's pie. He could smell it.

'Have you set the table?'

Charlie went on looking at her. The warm light, the

heat from the oven, the shepherd's pie, it all seemed to merge together into one block of extraordinary sensation, he was almost overwhelmed... and yet it made him so very happy, that she was still here, that dinner was almost ready.

But she was dead, wasn't she? She was definitely dead.

'Hug!' he stammered.

'What?'

'Hug!' He went towards her quickly with his arms outstretched, for he longed to hold onto her more than anything, and he knew too that this would be proof, beautiful proof, lasting evidence that the days he'd been living through had been some long, awful dream.

'You are a sweetheart aren't you!'

And sure enough, there she was, all big and warm and laughing at his silliness, wrapping her arms around him tightly.

'I love you, Nan!'

'I love you too, Charlie.'

From where his head was positioned, he could see the scrunched-up tissue she kept up her sleeve. It was pushed up right next to his eyes and he saw all the little folds and tears and details, and he could smell the strange soap she used, the pink block from her bathroom, the type Mum hated.

'But don't think this gets you out of laying the table!'

And so, they sat down together to eat, and they talked as they always did, about school, Charlie's parents, something Nan had seen on TV. It was all so wonderfully ordinary. At one moment, a break in the conversation, Charlie looked out through the curtains. He saw the bike against the lamppost and remembered.

'I thought you were a burglar! I saw the kitchen light. I thought it was a robber!'

She finished her mouthful.

'Why did you think that?'

'Because...' He was frowning, confused. 'Because I thought you were dead,' he whispered, looking at her uneasily, guiltily. 'I don't know why.'

She smiled at him caringly, with just a hint, a flicker of sadness. Then, as she pushed another piece of shepherd's pie onto the back of her fork, she said straightforwardly, '*Of course* I'm dead, Charlie.' She popped the food into her mouth. Charlie felt suddenly cold, and there were those nerves again, sparked into life, clawing at his insides like frantic hands.

'What?' he spluttered, 'Don't make jokes!' For a second, he hated her.

'Who's joking?' she asked.

'You are!'

'Charlie, don't be silly. You know that I'm dead.' It was as if it was some uninteresting, run of the mill thing. 'I fell over in the kitchen.' She might have been recalling some boring household chore. 'You know all this already.' Then, disapprovingly, 'Don't play the fool.'

He knew, of course, that it was true. He had always known. And then, for the first time, he felt that the tears would *really* come and there was nothing he could do, and he put his hands to his face as the great surge enveloped him, and shook him mercilessly, so much that he knocked against the table and all the things clattered. She was up immediately and by his side, holding him tightly again, trying to comfort, patting his back and saying, 'There, there,' a little flustered herself, clearly surprised and moved by this sudden turn.

Then they were on the sofa together. Charlie was quiet, tired from crying. Nan spoke gently.

'It happens to everyone, Charlie. You know that.'

He looked straight ahead. He heard his own voice, small and feeble.

'But ... I'm still sad. Really sad. All the time.'

'What about when you're riding your bike?' she asked.

He turned towards her.

'How do you know about my bike?'

'Of course, I know about you and your bike!'

He folded his arms.

'Well? You're not sad *all* the time. That's a fib, isn't it, Charles. I know you enjoy riding your bike.'

'*Most* of the time, then. Most of the time I'm really sad.' She had annoyed him by mentioning the bike. She was completely right of course, when he rode the bike he stopped feeling sad, or at least he felt less sad than usual, but here, now, he did not want to be reminded of that. He wanted to stay feeling sad, the depth and the pain of it was somehow reassuring. And he realised he felt guilty at the prospect of happiness.

'There's no need to feel guilty,' she told him.

'I don't...' he started, but stopped.

'When my own mother died, years ago, that's how I felt. I thought about her all the time, every second, it seemed. But sometimes, I'd catch myself thinking about something else. Not thinking about her. And the sadness had stopped, just for a moment. Like a little patch of sun showing through the rain clouds. And immediately I'd feel this awful guilt, as if I'd done something terrible, stopped loving her or something, stopped caring that she was gone. I thought it would upset her. I almost wanted to be sad. Isn't that a silly thing!' She looked at him knowingly over the top of her glasses. 'Wouldn't you agree?'

It did sound silly when she put it like that. But Charlie found that he could not say out loud that he agreed, as if a key had turned and his mouth was locked. To say she was right, the prospect of it almost... frightened him.

'Of course, everyone goes through the same sort of thing. It takes a bit of time, and that's alright. After a while you'll be ready, Charlie, don't you worry about that!'

'Ready for what?' he asked quietly. He did not like her calmness in her voice at all. He fidgeted and his mouth wobbled.

She was smiling now, so warm and with such love. 'Ready to be happy again, of course!'

He had started to cry again, though not loudly this time, and he found that he was still able to speak a bit through the tears.

'I just feel sorry for you,' he told her.

And then, peculiarly, she laughed. A short, instinctive laugh. He didn't understand.

'Oh, Charlie! Of course you don't!'

That annoyed him.

'I DO!'

She looked a little more seriously at him.

'No, Charlie. You don't.'

Her response had surprised him so much that he'd stopped crying.

'What...?'

'I haven't broken a bone. Or... had my things stolen

by burglars. *Then* you might feel sorry for me. But I'm *dead*. It's very different. Totally different in fact. I don't exist. You can't feel sorry for someone that doesn't exist. It doesn't make sense.' She was speaking in that matter of fact tone again. 'Think about it.'

Charlie was frowning again. He thought about it. He *did* feel sorry for her, didn't he?

'You don't,' she insisted.

He considered the examples she'd given, the broken bone and the burglar, and thought of her hobbling about on crutches, or powerless to resist as robbers took all her precious things. Her sad face afterwards. Living through it.

'That's it,' she said, encouragingly.

And then he closed his eyes and tried to think of her *now*, now that she was dead... but somehow, he could not think of her, or rather he didn't know where to place her, how her face would look, because that was just it, she was gone, she wasn't anywhere. He gasped and opened his eyes.

'The only person you feel sorry for is you, Charlie. And that's alright. After all, it's not a nice thing you've been through. Worse than a broken bone, I'd say!'

All the time she was smiling, and the warm lights in the room seemed soft and beautiful, like an old painting. Charlie sat closer to his grandmother and they put their arms around each other once more. He didn't speak. He was not happy yet. The panging grief was still there, and he missed her terribly. He felt tired. But something had changed. She did not exist, he knew that. And if she did not exist, then she could feel no unhappiness, no fear. So there was no reason, as she'd told him, to feel sorry for her. He did not need to worry about her. He could feel the bump in her sleeve where she always kept that tissue. He even heard her breathing.

And he *did* feel sorry for himself. Why should he have to go through something as horrible as this? He was only eleven. But, he realised, the nerves that had troubled him through all of those days, the nerves that had worn him out and stopped him eating... they had gone. Like a great flock of birds, disturbed by some sound or change in the air, they'd taken off, as one, and were far away now, still in view but only just, a million specks on the shoreline, soaring and pulsing. Distant. Charlie watched them for a moment more, and then, when he was ready... turned away.

# Love

# FOOD

# Blackberry Picking

## Brigitte de Valk

The silk chiffon of summer had fallen away. Autumn was revealed, nude and cold. There was a sense of relief. The gaiety of the previous season was over, and the fields of the countryside were saturated in subtle brown hues. It was October. The earth could finally breathe.

Belle shivered. She could feel the uneven texture of the ground beneath her boots. Cows had trodden along the path when the soil had been wet, and their hooves had left deep groove marks. There was a metallic quality to the air, like the must of old copper pennies found at the back of a drawer.

A carrier bag full of empty tin cans rustled and clinked as Belle walked. It formed a musical accompaniment to each long stride she took. She glanced up as she entered a new field. The sky was a stark pale grey, with muscular clouds that bulged, almost touching the ground in the far distance. Smoke, from a bonfire, fled into the sky and quickly disappeared. Dead branches and shrubberies were being burnt. Belle paused and took a deep breath. Her heartbeat was uneven. The thought of death was too prescient.

'Blackberries,' Belle murmured.

She cleared her throat. An image of Seamus Heaney bloomed in her mind. She imagined the gentle gravitas of his voice as he recited poetry. There was a dark warmth to his eyes. Ever since her father died, Belle had sought the paternal elsewhere. She crouched down and placed her palm against dry earth. She crumbled a little soil between her fingertips. Her father had never looked at her directly when he spoke. His gaze flitted about the room, alighting nervously here and there. His pupils were trapped blackbirds, encircled by a hazel ring.

Belle stood. She redid the top button of her coat. The muscles in her legs ached quietly; she had been walking for hours. There were pink marks on her hands from where the plastic handle of the bag had cut. She thought of the way her father had talked to her, through gesticulation, mostly, and subtle facial movements. He hummed a little, and when he did speak, his voice was soothing and rough, like the texture of recently chopped wood. Communication solely through words seemed a bereft approach to language. Besides, Belle had never prioritised sentences strung beautifully together. She was averse to the hierarchy of fluid prose. She preferred the dark crackle of the fire at night, or the sound of her heart, beating dimly within her constricted chest.

There was a dull glamour to the sky now. A touch of gold had appeared on the horizon. Belle began to walk, her pace a little quicker. Her tastes were changing. She was turning to poetry to fill the silence her father had left. Perhaps Heaney was a good place for her to start. He seemed to invite certain cadences to his words, like underground rivers, flowing invisibly. Belle surveyed the hedgerows. She could spy the black fruit she was after, but there was an adamant, almost superstitious, spark in her that led her further onward to a particular grove she wanted to pluck from. There was an elusive quality to Heaney, as with her father. Nature had whispered intimate secrets into their ears as they slept.

Belle pushed open the cold iron of a gate. It groaned in lament. She re-bolted it, a slight tremor to her fingers – they were growing numb. Her knuckles protruded, a harsh-red, like small mountains against the rest of her skin.

Belle straightened and turned around. She had arrived; this was the field. It was deserted. The soil had been tilled into neat rows that stretched endlessly away. She neared the bramble hedges where clots of dark fruit clung to their branches. A smile passed over Belle's face, like sunlight glancing through a thick cloudscape. Blackberries in autumn were latecomers to a dying party. They were the last piquant sting before the season shriveled into a colder, drab version of itself.

Belle's hand reached forward, and her fingertips clumsily picked a cluster of berries. She dropped them soundlessly into a tin. She was too cold to feel the pinpricks of the thorns. Again, she navigated the intricate web of branches and drew forth black, edible gold. The tins soon filled.

A tear threatened to spill at the edge of her eye. She blinked it away. The noise of cows lowing could be heard in a memory that surfaced. It coupled with the opaque silhouette of her father, walking in the distance, his shoulders stooped. Belle pressed her lips together. She concentrated on the inky gloss of the berries; anticipation of their sharp flavour drummed in the air.

Coal dust lingered on Belle's palms. The scrape of a shovel ceased, the iron bucket was full enough. Belle leant the shovel against the side of the stone shed and clapped her hands together, trying to dislodge the dirt. The scent of mould filled her nostrils. It was peaceful here. The shed felt like a go-between, between the exterior and the interior world. The wild unknowability of nature was mirrored in the crevices and shadows of its walls. It possessed an inherent discomfort and cold; with its fine lines of web intricately wrought in all four corners. And yet, Belle straightened and wrapped her fingers around the handle of the bucket, the shed pertained a gentle hush, that could not exist outside. She heard each faint breath she took, shallow yet regular.

Belle paused on her route back to the kitchen. Night burgeoned swiftly, and she inhaled the refreshing dark of the air, fertile as soil. Vines viciously ribboned themselves through the garden. Discarded tools were vague outlines as water dripped sedately into a metal dish. It provided an iron echo.

This was once her father's favourite time of day. He felt vitalised by the shadowed beauty of nocturnality, the pressure of expectation fell from his narrow frame. He would call his daughter into the living room, and they would sit together with the windows wide open, even in winter. Belle would be wrapped in a blanket, while her father simply wore his long coat. They kept an oath of silence and listened to the indistinct noise of night-time.

The kitchen bled a mellow rectangle of gold. Belle entered and closed the door behind her. She carefully stepped out of her boots and placed the coal bucket on the tiles. She rinsed her hands in the sink, turning the water dark and then clear. Mounds of blackberries littered the counter tops, they sat in saucepans and colanders, bowls, and mugs. The berries gleamed with water droplets; they were irresistible, brain-like, thorned.

Belle placed a berry in the palm of her hand. She rolled it around with the tip of her forefinger, and then let it drop into the basin of the sink. Its skin felt smooth, as though polished with nature's sweat. Heaney had watched his blackberry riches disintegrate into a rat-grey fungus. As a boy, he had experienced a hot flush of disappointment. The concept of beauty's death lingered at the back of his throat as he read his poems aloud. His words caught on this grief, like a match being struck, providing a guttural acknowledgement of nature's brutality.

Belle flicked off the kitchen lights.

The white of the hospital pillow drained what little colour remained in her father's face. His eyelids twitched haphazardly. The tangle of his wrinkles, deeply etched, seemed to rebel against the neat order of the room. Belle had stood by the window, her elbow on the sill, watching the curtains flutter. They were made of delicate gauze. Her father was fading away. She could feel this somehow, and her only thoughts were of regret. He shouldn't die here. His last breath should take place outside. Her fingers tried to pry open the window, but it was locked. A faint scent of disinfectant edged around the corners of the room.

Burgundy carnations were arranged untidily in a vase. Belle avoided looking at them. Their petals reminded her of dried blood.

The corridor echoed with footsteps, and frustration fluttered in her chest, but then, calmed, like leaves settling on the ground. Her father's hand rested on his chest. It was a limp, pale thing, moving up and down with the rhythm of his weak diaphragm. She memorised its every contour and freckle until her vision grew blurred.

Belle's childhood bedroom rippled with shadows as she slipped under the bedcovers. The sheets were cold and soothing. An aged bear lay next to her pillow; her eyes remained open. The mattress creaked a little.

There was an elegiac quality to the blackberries, who remained silent downstairs, dressed in mourning. Words failed. Or at least they had at the funeral. Belle's throat had become choked with lacklustre words. She had stood at the church pulpit, looking down at the oval faces that stared back at her, and she couldn't utter a thing. Eventually, someone led her down and sat her on a wooden pew. Ringing had filled her ears. Her father's casket was unadorned.

Belle closed her eyes. Dreams began to orientate themselves around her last conscious thoughts. Soon, the night deepened into something electric. Belle stood barefoot on a barren field. She was painting with blackberry juice: a naked body formed on a large canvas. It was a silhouette she was familiar with. Belle peered at it closely, and goosepimples formed along her shoulders. She realised the canvas was a mirror. She was nude. The outline in the glass could no longer contain the feeling that broiled in her veins. It began to merge with the clouds reflected in the background. Belle stepped forward.

She awoke with a gasp. After a moment, she turned over and fell into a quieter sleep.

Coffee filled her mouth. The charcoal aftereffects of dawn laced themselves across the sky while Belle sat on the kitchen step; her palms warmed by the mug. A few brown sparrows rustled in a tall tree. Heaney's voice resounded quietly from a speaker. It filled her with a calm acceptance. His poems perfectly fit the wooden grooves of her memories, and the knots that formed where branches had once been. Morning broke gently on the horizon.

She wore her father's long coat, draped over her shoulders.

# Breadcrumbs

## Molly Smith Main

She looked down at the blank screen with its cursor flashing anxiously in dismay. What did she want to say? 'Help, I'm so lonely!' sounded a little dramatic, and although honest, it didn't seem quite positive enough to make any friends. She scrolled down slowly, pressing the tiny heart-shaped button robotically. Photo after photo of beautifully drawn eyebrows arched over thickly lashed eyes looking away from her and towards some perfect life.

Search #womansfashion

Glancing down at her worn leggings, she unhelpfully smudged a stray speck of tomato soup down her leg. 'What can I say that is going to be even remotely interesting to anybody on here?' She'd had her clothes for ages, and every time she attempted to put on make-up, she ended up looking like a cheap drag artist. Her daughter had been the one who had suggested she create an Instagram account. Pearl posted a photo every day and said it would be a lovely way of seeing what the grandchildren were up to. It had taken her a while to get used to it- all these buttons and scrolling were slightly different from the typewriter she had learned on at school, but now she had the hang of it; she loved seeing their smiling faces and what they had been up to. She wished she could see more of them, but they lived so far away.

Search #missinggrandchildren

She frowned as she scrolled past a photo of a bowl

of food, broccoli and sweetcorn, something black and some rice. She was still completely confused about why people thought it was remarkable that they had made some food. She tried to imagine collecting a fat packet of photographs from Boots, after anxiously waiting for a few days, only to be greeted by plates of beans on toast, bowls of cornflakes and a mug of tea.

Search- #whydopeoplepostpicturesoffood?

Pearl had thought Instagram might help her make friends - friends in her phone as she called them - as she didn't get out much anymore, especially now. She had only spoken face to face with one person this week, and that was Will at the paper shop when she had run out of teabags. She couldn't remember when she'd become so isolated and introverted? Perhaps when she had left the factory four years ago after over 30 years of service- she missed her colleagues there, missed their chats in the tea-room and the feeling of camaraderie as they put on their aprons and hairnets and trooped into the 'oven' as they called it. Dr Jacob had suggested she 'get out more.' But where was she to go?

Search #getoutmore

It was 11.00 am, time for her morning mug of tea. This Instagram could take up the whole morning if she let it. She sat at her kitchen table, looking out the window at the trees at the bottom of her garden. Her Dad had planted that apple tree before her elder brothers and her were born. They had loved eating the apples and climbing in the branches if their Mum wasn't looking.

After lunch finished at 1.00 pm sharp, she put on the radio, pulled her apron over her head, and began making her bread. She had always loved the smell of fresh bread ever since her father had come home from the bakery with a warm white loaf wrapped in crunchy brown paper. Her Mum had coarsely sliced the loaf, and they would all sit around the kitchen table stuffing chunks of soft bread dripping with melting margarine into their hungry mouths. She tipped out the mix and began to push and fold, squash, and knead the warm, pliable dough. As she squished, she thought back to when her daughter was little, how she had played happily in the street, laughing loudly and crying for attention when she had fallen over or was hungry. She'd had to work hard at the time, juggling work and family but never realised just how lucky she was to have all her loved ones around her. She had adored being a mum, keeping her baby safe and warm, listening to her read and encouraging Pearl to keep learning. She had told her stories every night before bedtime. One of their favourite stories was Hansel and Gretel. She'd always thought Hansel was so clever to leave a little trail of breadcrumbs so they could find the way back. She smiled when she remembered her daughters' squeals of delight as she read about the witch in her cottage in the woods. She wondered now if the witch was just a lonely, old woman. Stuck in her house looking out at the trees, pleased for some young company and smiling faces.

Search #lonelywoman

Well, blimey, that was a search she wasn't going to try again.

She'd been ever so proud when her daughter had gone to university. She was the first person from the family to go, and her degree had meant she had been able to get a good job - it was just a shame she had moved so far away as she'd have loved to be able to help to look after the kids.

Search #grandma

Since she was no longer working, she had sorted through all her clothes and washed and mended the ones she wore. She scrolled once again through photos of glossy haired woman, teeth so white they almost looked blue, wearing tiny, figure-hugging dresses and huge, towering heels clutching branded patent bags and enormous sunglasses as they jetted off to some exotic, luxury holiday. She'd been on holiday a few times but never left England. Her late husband hadn't wanted to travel, but they had saved up and gone to Bournemouth a few times. She had loved the feel of the sun and sand on her skin. They had stayed in a B&B looking over Boscombe Pier, somehow fish and chips tasted even better at the seaside. It had been three years now since he had gone. The house was too quiet without him.

Search #matureladiesfashion

Ah, that was a bit more like it- there were pictures of 'real' people- wearing 'normal' clothes. Also, a few interesting posts about women her age. Silver-haired ladies. Even a post about 'empowering women' She wondered if she had ever been empowered. The famous Bread Shortages of 1977? She had stood outside the factory with her pal, Sue and all their workmates, waving their placards, striking for extra money. Sue had died last winter after suffering from throat cancer. They had all felt powerful when they returned to work and were given a few pounds extra in their wage packet. Felt rather daring now.

As she walked through the hall, she caught a glimpse of herself in the mirror. Her hair was a yellowing grey as she neared her 70th year. She had kept it long and usually wore it tied in a ponytail, just had she had when she was younger and had to keep it tucked in a net cap for the factory. The radio was playing a song by The Beatles, and she suddenly felt like a teenager again. She carefully hauled the loaf out of the oven and set it on a cooling rack. It was a thing of beauty. The golden crust glistened in the light from the window, and the smell was amazing. She decided to take a photo of it and send it to Pearl. The grandchildren had always loved her bread too. After a few attempts, one of which involved her getting a rather disturbing photo of herself with what looked like a huge chin, she got one she was happy with and sent it off to Pearl.

'Wow! Mum, that looks like a delicious loaf!! Jack and Meg would love some of that! I'll post it on your Instagram page! #artisanbread - Take care, see you soon! P xxx'

The next morning, she switched her phone on. A little red circle was on her Instagram button. When she clicked on it, she saw the photo of her bread had had over 836 likes. There were so many comments and questions, too- This looks amazing! How Did you make this? I wish I could do that! Can I have the recipe? You've inspired me to bake bread! How did you get the crust so golden? Mine never looks like that! And 127 people wanted to follow her – whatever that meant.

# Molding Sonnet

Milie Fiirgaard Rasmussen

Shall I compare us to a sourdough?
So rare and tepid, kneading your embrace.
We stir and bend as bodies fit a mold,
while heat do rise 'round shivers to erase.
A push past lines, entwined; yet not all spoken
with syrup voice, call quaint lit streets a home.
With acts of scoring; flesh calmly opened.
Short breathing revealing the shells' shy moan.
Our walls of steal seal stress and mess away.
This pot lid that did fit nicely, until
it touched the crust. We clean another day.
Ferment; content with spots, we see them still
  as heat so sweet can carry voices clear:
  To grow and learn, I burn and stand still here.

# MINDFULNESS

# Asylum

Anna Seidel

Crossing my lips, you trace each crest, crease, bend,
the branch jabbed soles of my bifid tongue,
feel thin mountain air sped breath-beats;

Explore raw paths plied in soil, riptides of my mouth,
where prayers of poison, prayers of thorns
near childhood dreams rest;

Where secret thoughts silently take seed,
cradling lost roots on taste buds,
hiding a grief finely sewn into flesh.

Did you find the words that had flout borders,
smuggled in the cavities of my wisdom teeth, tunnels
through which memory haunts my mind
like an endless reverberating tremor?
Did you ever have to measure a word's ballast?

These exiled idioms held so much for so long.
Wrapped in sheepskin, vowels brimming,
their lettered backs broken from all the weight.

In each cavern of a kiss, I search foreign words
to re-sculpt my story from, seek harbour
in strange tongues, that so often fail to hold.

# Wildfires

## CosMos

Our emotions are like small wildfires,
sometimes they can destroy and consume us
yet sometimes they have the power to rebuild
worlds.

# The Post-Pandemic Thirst

C. L. Cooke

Squashed in between a future world and tired old existence
Although grateful for past teachings, we need to prosper now
Longing for a different road; fresh faces with assistance
Now know we too may offer, loan of our wise brows
If it is decided courage derives from aged worn- out fears
Aid is freely gifted, travellers dry our stricken tears
We shall seek out all forgotten gifts that make said paths unique
And feel the weight of gratitude from events occurred last week
We'll have a lonely moment or two or three or ten
Whilst we figure out how to advance our mighty strength again
There is space for us to fit, albeit inside new rooms
Where the seats are unfamiliar and unforeseen experience looms
The people we will find, we've already beckoned
From decisions and mistakes that have been diarised and reckoned
Said learning curves are not all harsh and some are even sweet

They're the fruit of recent efforts where fate and longing meet
Thirst to harness moments that promote the meaningful
Containing truth and banishing the closed off and the dull
Whoever you may be; unmet folk in unmet places
We'll convene us there, fully ready, wholly gracious.

# Carlow Poem #77

Derek Coyle

Someday I'll tune up my cello
and sit in the middle
of the Bog of Allen, my music stand
before me, the wind
my page turner.
I'll play Kodály's 'Sonata for Solo Cello'
in honour of all the dead trees.
I can see the notes wafting
out across the June evening,
like peaceful midges dancing.
It will be a song of praise too.
For all the carbon this bog
is going to soak up in a final
act of usefulness on our behalf.
Ah yes, hear those resonant notes,
that deep bass. And then,
when I'm done,
I'll make a small raft
out of broken pallets. Some boys
from Raheendoran will give me a hand,
so that I can sail down the Barrow,
this time playing Britten, Benjamin Britten,
the slow bowing of my cello
a dirge for all the dead salmon,
all the fish lost to this river.
Maybe it's not quite dead yet,
but from one point of view
it's near extinction. I'll play my dirge

the way church bells ring out
over a village, hoping
some will stop, listen and think,
and maybe see a mallard duck
move sideways across the water,
thoughtfully getting out of the way
of a young salmon,
heading eagerly downstream,
on its way to sea.
Meanwhile, the willows are all ears,
in a curious silence.

# The Owl Man

## S. P. Thane

Did you ever hear of The Owl Man?
WHO?
The Owl Man!
WHO?
Who is The Owl Man, to whom it may concern?

He who does not hide
He only lives in the hood of night
He walks with thoughts, wonders and ponders
On top of the trees and everything under

So, have you heard of The Owl Man?
The Who?
The Owl Man!
The Who?
No, The Owl Man, although I like their tunes
Who is the The Owl Man, to whom it may concern?

Who we may see and who he may be
The question of whom, he does not speak?
He has some teeth, but has no beak
Some have seen him, but only a peek
Is he alive if he only walks the dead of night?

So, have you heard of The Owl Man?
WHO?
The Owl Man!
WHO?

Who is The Owl Man, to whom it may concern?

They say to him the word of man lost all meaning
So, what is the point in ever speaking
A hermit, a nomad what if he is no man?
A traveller, a vagabond
A simple searcher who looks from beyond

So, who is The Owl Man?
So, you really do not know?
No! Who is the who of who you speak?
Who is the Owl Man, to me it may concern?

He is a whom's who of who to whom it may concern.

Mindfulness

# A Word About Our Writers

## Sharon Black

Sharon Black is from Glasgow and lives in a remote valley of the Cévennes mountains. Her poetry is published widely and has won many prizes. Her collections are *To Know Bedrock* (Pindrop, 2011), *The Art of Egg* (Two Ravens, 2015; Pindrop, 2019), and a pamphlet, *Rib* (Wayleave, 2021). Her third and fourth full collections will appear in 2022 with *Vagabond Voices* and *Drunk Muse Press* respectively.

www.sharonblack.co.uk

## Everett Jay Buchanan

Everett is a third-year scriptwriting student at Bournemouth University. He is Bulgarian and grew up in the country's capital, Sofia. Everett started writing when he was ten years old and dreamt of being a novelist, albeit that he's directed those ambitions at being a screenwriter instead. He often draws inspiration from popular media and music. Everett does drag in his free time and is often informed by this in his writing.

## C. L. Cooke

Claire has written poems and short stories since the age of seven. She is now a few anniversaries past her 35th birthday and has chosen 2022 to be her publishing year! She is two thirds through her first novel, (Suspense and Difference being the key themes). As a poet she has derived inspiration from Ted Hughes, (living a stone's throw from his birth place).

## CosMos

CosMos is a poet, writer, and visual artist. Her poems have been published in the UK and abroad in literary magazines. The themes of her work explore inner worlds, nature, the cosmos, the universe, and the natural world. Her inspiration is drawn from these places daily as she collects musings, observations, and realizations which she also accompanies with visual imagery through painting and collage.

She is currently a student in contemporary art at Bath Spa University.

## Martin Costello

Martin Costello is an educator, social entrepreneur and performer based in Nottinghamshire. Via a circuitous route through community activism, arts leadership, a doctorate in philosophy, and teaching, he is founder and principal of a therapeutic school for trauma-affected teenagers, director of educational and environmental social enterprises and Churchill Fellow. Well-known on the local spoken word scene performing as Another Poet, he also hosts events including a slam week at the 2018 Nottingham UNESCO poetry festival.

## Derek Coyle

Derek Coyle published his first collection, *Reading John Ashbery in Costa Coffee Carlow* in a dual-language edition in Tranas Sweden and Carlow Ireland in April 2019, and it was shortlisted for the Shine Strong 2020 poetry award. He lectures in Carlow College/St Patrick's, Ireland. His forthcoming collection *Sipping Martinis under Mount Leinster* will be published in the Summer 2022.

## Niamh Donnellan

Niamh Donnellan is a writer from Meath, Ireland. Working in communications, she shares other people's stories for a living. Outside office hours, she writes her own. She won the Anthology Short Story Competition 2020 and was selected for the XBorders 2019 and 2020 projects with the Irish Writers Centre. As well as writing a novel, she is currently finishing her first collection of short stories and dabbling in poetry.

## Roan Ellis-O'Neill

Roan Ellis-O'Neill is a writer and poet from Belfast. His work features in Hold Open the Door and Interdisciplinary Literary Studies. In 2021, he co-created Placing Poems, an online, interactive map offering a chance to write about new and imagined journeys away from the stifling reality of the pandemic, with cartographer Ceren Dolma.

## Felix Fennell

Felix Fennell is a self-taught artist and writer, who spent his childhood travelling between countries, the effects of which are sometimes reflected in his characters. He graduated university studying Religion and Ethics, and believes the three years spent studying there hold some of his fondest memories. When he isn't attempting to weave together stories, he enjoys raising cacti and indulging his sweet tooth. His fundamental philosophy is that there is always something more to learn from the world.

## Milie Fiirgaard Rasmussen

Milie is a young woman fascinated by identity and culture. Having spent her teenage years in a small Danish town, she started searching for cultures to explore. As such, she now studies Creative Writing and Publishing at Bournemouth University where she gets to fully explore her creative interests and develop her poetic skills. Her poetry often has the linguistic rhythms of a language nerd, and reflects personal emotions and memories.

## Michael Gaines

Michael Gaines is a fiction writer from Poole, Dorset. He has a BA in Performing Arts, as well as an MA in Creative Writing and Publishing from Bournemouth University. He is currently a student of PhD in Media and Communication, researching the impact that ancient stories have on the production of modern narratives. He most enjoys writing fantasy and science fiction, and believes that art is the purest expression of emotion that a person can offer the world.

'Autumn Skies' was inspired by the sad passing of Stephen Sondheim, and is a response to the influence that certain individuals can have on our world. It is dedicated to the many legends we have lost in recent years, and is a story of reflection, acceptance, appreciation, and hope for the future.

## Dale Hurst

Dale Hurst is an English novelist, poet, journalist, and broadcaster. As a writer, he specialises in historical and mystery fiction.

Having dabbled in writing in various formats since he was ten, he published his first novel, the mystery The Berylford Scandals: Lust & Liberty in 2018. A sequel, Sin & Secrecy, followed in 2020.

Dale is also the presenter of The Dale Hurst Writing Show, a podcast discussing issues surrounding writing, publishing, and storytelling.

## Laila Lock

Laila Lock is currently studying for a Master's degree in Creative Writing at Bournemouth University. She lives with her family and an eclectic range of animals in Dorset

## Bernie McQuillan

Bernie McQuillan's short stories have been both published and placed in a number of competitions, including semi-finalist in The Machigonne Fiction contest 2018 (publication in The New Guard Vol 8 in 2019); Leicester Writes Short Story competition 2018; Emerald Street's short story competition; long listed in the Fish Flash Fiction Award 2015 and shortlisted in both Creative Writing.ie & Creative Writing.uk. Stories have been published in Woman's Way magazine, The Incubator (3 stories), Spontaneity, The Honest Ulsterman, Birmingham Arts Journal (US), the Leicester Writes Anthology 2018 and The New Guard 2019. Bernie lives in Belfast.

## Molly Smith Main

Molly studied Drama and History of Art at university. As well as writing short stories and poetry, her passions are genealogy, history, preloved clothes, painting and reading in her spare time. She completed her MA in Creative Writing and Publishing at Bournemouth University. She lives in a quirky old house stuffed with over 1000 books and is happily married with two daughters.

## Nikki Nova

Nikki Nova lives in England where she writes. She is also working as a restaurant general manager. Her favorite part of her job is being surrounded by many different people and getting her inspiration from them. Burning whispers is Nikki Nova's first poetry collection that will be published in 2022 by Bookleaf publishing house. Her poem 'Home' got published in The Waves of Change Bournemouth Writing Prize 2021 anthology.

## Bradley Petrie

Bradley Petrie is a final year student at Bournemouth University. Throughout his degree he has been able to write two short pieces of fiction which he is very proud of. After hearing about the Bournemouth Writers Prize for his final writing assignment, he was excited to submit them and enter the competition himself in hopes of his work being recognised professionally.

## Tim Relf

Tim Relf is a Leicestershire-based writer working on his first collection. His poems have appeared – or are forthcoming – in The Rialto, The Frogmore Papers, One Hand Clapping, Wild Court, The Friday Poem, Ink Sweat & Tears and Snakeskin. He was runner-up in the 2021 McLellan Poetry Competition. His latest novel, published by Penguin, has been translated into more than 20 languages. He also contributes to Poetry News and BookBrunch.

## Helen Ribchester

Helen is an Occupational Therapy lecturer with an interest in the value of poetry as a tool to express thoughts, feelings, reflections and understanding both personally, professionally and within academic work. After several years of struggling, the discovery and inclusion of poetry in academic writing has transformed her approach to her doctoral studies and liberated her ability to articulate her thoughts and ideas.

## Bill Richardson

Bill Richardson is Emeritus Professor in Spanish at the National University of Ireland Galway. Poems of his have been published in Irish newspapers, as well as in Atrium, The Galway Review, Vox Galvia, The Seventh Quarry, Amethyst Review, The Stony Thursday Book and the Fish Anthology 2020.

## Sharon Savvas

Sharon Savvas is a New Zealand writer who divides her life between New Zealand, England and Cyprus. Sharon was shortlisted for The Bridport Prize, Kilmore Literary Festival Write by the Sea, Allingham Festival in 2021, and longlisted for Sligo Cairde Short Story Award, Flash500.

Sharon was nominated for the 2020 Pushcart, and has been published online in anthologies and magazines.

## Anna Seidel

Anna Seidel is currently completing her MSt in Creative Writing at the University of Oxford alongside a career in economics. She previously read business economics and philosophy at the University of St. Gallen, Switzerland and at Harvard University. Also, she is the co-founder of the poetry foundation 'The Napkin Poetry Review'. Her poetic work has been published in Stanford University's Literature Journal *Mantis, Stand, The Fiddlehead, Brittle Star, Inkwell, Marble Poetry,* and *Frontier Poetry*, among others.

## Martyn Smiles

Originally from London, Martyn Smiles has written poetry and short stories for a number of years, being both an avid reader and an avid writer. He resides happily in Ireland among the green and rolling hills, an ideal setting for a contemplative writer.

## Peter R. Storey

Peter Storey teaches English and academic skills (including writing) to international students at the University of Cambridge. Originally from Yorkshire, his passions include music, running, swimming, languages, nature, and travel. A keen composer of music, as well as words, his creative work tends to explore themes linked to particular periods of history or to the natural world.

## S. P. Thane

S. P. Thane is an active poet, lyricist, vlogger, writer and podcast host. He engages in many variants of writing when it comes to story telling through his short stories, manga/comics, poetry, music and other amongst those.

S. P. Thane's main themes in writing blend much of real world experience with that of metaphorical fantasy. Attempting to gage current and new readers with his diverse style.

## Henry Tydeman

Henry is an English tutor. In 2021 his short story 'The Pigeons' was shortlisted in the Wild Hunt Magazine prize, and another of his stories was chosen for publication in the *Manchester Review*. His short plays have been performed by the New Works Playhouse. He has also written about politics and the arts for Huffington Post and Reaction.

## Brigitte de Valk

Brigitte de Valk is the winner of the Cúirt New Writing Prize 2020 (adjudicated by Claire-Louise Bennett) and the Royal Holloway Art Writing Competition. She was awarded second place in the Benedict Kiely Short Story Competition and was longlisted for The Alpine Fellowship Writing Prize 2020. Her entry to the Bournemouth Writing Prize 2021 was selected for publication. Brigitte's short fiction is also published by Happy London Press and Reflex Press.

## Acknowledgements

As a team, we'd like to send a massive thank you to the Bournemouth University Creative Writing and Publishing staff for their technical support and guidance, to our fellow editors at Fresher Publishing, and most importantly to the authors, without whom this book would not have been possible.

Printed in Great Britain
by Amazon